DAWN OF AN EMPIRE

SINS Series Book 4

EMMA SLATE

©2017 by Tabula Rasa Publishing, Inc.
All rights reserved.

No part of this publication may be reproduced, distributed or transmitted in any form or by any means, including photocopying, recording, or other electronic or mechanical methods, without the prior written permission of the publisher, except in the case of brief quotations embodied in critical reviews and certain other noncommercial uses permitted by copyright law.

This book is a work of fiction. Names, characters, places, and incidents are the product of the author's imagination or are used fictitiously. Any resemblance to actual events, locales, or persons, living or dead, is coincidental.

For the Villains.

Prologue

He stood outside the bedroom door, the instrument case clutched in his small hands. Pressing his ear to wood, he listened and waited. There were no sounds of raised voices or tired pleas, only the light, raspy breathing of a woman slowly dying.

After raising his hand to knock, he stilled. He loved and loathed these moments. Loathed because the room smelled of lingering death that no amount of fresh air or incense sticks disguised. Loved because of the woman in the bed.

"Rybka," she called. Her voice was weak, as thin as an ancient scroll about to crumble to dust.

He turned the knob and entered the bedroom, shutting the door behind him. He didn't dare lock it.

"Come here." She attempted to lift her hand to him, but the effort was too great, and it fell back to her side. It was pale, milky, and the blue veins under her skin were as delicate as spider legs.

Her once burnished copper hair was now lank, faded, and thin. She'd been a great beauty, a classic profile in a no-longer-classic world. Still, others had recognized her for what she was—old glamour and charm. She moved like a dancer, but carried herself like a queen.

"Play something for me, *rybka*, my little fish," she begged through chapped lips.

He set the battered instrument case on the floor and opened it to reveal a viola. Gently lifting the instrument, he gazed at it in worshipful reverence. He brought it to the bed, lifted her hand, and helped her stroke the wooden body.

"My great-great-grandfather came to this country with nothing—nothing except this viola," she said.

He'd heard the story more than a dozen times, but it was his favorite, and he listened with rapt attention as though it was the first. Her blue eyes lit up as she recounted the tale.

"You do him a great honor, *rybka*. You will play for audiences who will rise to their feet to pay you tribute. You will be beloved for your music. Play for me," she repeated.

"What would you like to hear?" he asked.

"Your choice, today."

He took the viola and placed it under his chin. Without taking his eyes off her, he played a song he composed. A joyful, uplifting melody that brought a smile to her lips. He continued to play for hours, long after the sun had set. She was a most enthusiastic spectator, and though she was too exhausted to clap, her words of praise were all the validation he needed.

The front door slamming against the wall popped their happy, insulated bubble. A raised voice, yelling in Russian, the sounds of shoes thumping against furniture.

"Hurry. Don't let him find you in here, *rybka*."

He quickly shoved the viola into its case and then snapped the lid shut. The footsteps were coming up the stairs.

"Under the bed. Now."

It was a tale as old as time: a child hiding, praying not to be found, wishing he could block out the angry words spewing from his embittered father. It was nothing more than fear—fear that he would soon lose his wife and be left in this rotten world alone without her, forced to raise a child he didn't understand.

Cheek pressed to the battered viola case, the child fell asleep to the sound of his father weeping.

Chapter 1

Igor Dolinsky stared out the window and watched snow falling in the dark night. He clutched a glass of vodka in his hand. The memory burned bright and hot in his mind and no matter how many years passed, no matter how many women, no matter how much vodka, he couldn't ever forget the smell of death. It lingered in his nose; it imprinted on his mind.

Her warm fingers trailed up his back before she wrapped her arms around his waist. "Come back to bed," she invited.

Three hours ago, when he'd met her at the bar, he'd been eager, ready, savage. She'd pretended to be afraid, but her obvious desire for his brutal lust was just a facade. Now, he was only marginally sated, and he wanted his bed empty, the fake blonde vixen gone from his home.

"Not tired." He swirled the contents of his glass, ice clinking.

"Who said anything about sleeping?" Her hand drifted lower until she grasped him. She tugged and caressed until he swelled. "Hmm," she moaned against his back. "You're ready for more."

He threw back the rest of his vodka and set the glass down. His hand gently clasped her wrist.

She released him.

He turned and was on her before she had a chance to utter a protest—which she wouldn't have done.

He took her on the floor, fast and furious, not at all mindful of her pleasure. A rutting beast, he grunted and groaned. She arched into him and scratched his back with her too long nails.

If she came, he didn't care.

He came, hard.

Empty. Always so empty.

Her hands went to his hair as she tried to get him to kiss her.

He wouldn't oblige.

She pouted and it made him look at her in disgust. He wanted to ask her why she didn't value herself, why her makeup was on just a touch too heavy, why her hair a shade too bright. But he didn't because that would mean he gave a damn.

And he didn't give a damn about anything.

Lifting himself off her, he looked around for his cell phone.

"What are you doing?" she asked, stretching her arms up over her head.

"Calling you a car."

She blinked. "I could stay."

"I sleep alone."

"You're fucked up."

"*Da.* And you're vulgar."

She slithered into her clothes and had the audacity to be offended.

Igor shook his head in disbelief. When a woman went home with a man on the first night of meeting, what was he to think of her? There was no pretense; he hadn't promised her a thing.

"I'll walk you out," he said, slipping into his wrinkled and discarded clothes.

"Don't bother." She sneered. "I can see myself out."

He shrugged.

Apathy from a man pissed a woman off more than anything else.

On her way out, she chucked her lipstick case at him. He didn't bother ducking since it sailed wide.

"Get some therapy," she snapped. The front door slammed, and all was silent in the Battery Park penthouse. He locked up, just in case she came back in a streak of vengeance.

Igor poured himself another glass of vodka and sat down in a comfortable, plush chair. His cell phone rang not five minutes later. He debated letting it go to voicemail and then dismissed the idea. Olaf wouldn't be pleased if Igor ignored his call.

"*Da*," he said into his cell.

"That is how you greet me?" Olaf demanded.

Igor didn't engage. He waited.

"Is it done?" Olaf asked, hatred blooming in his voice.

"Of course."

"Meeting tomorrow. Do not be late." Olaf hung up without waiting for Igor's insubordination that would never come.

At ten years old, Igor had learned how to bury everything that mattered to him. Sometimes he forgot there were pieces of himself he didn't share with the world. Not anymore. It was easier to leave them in the past with his dead mother. Easier to conceal them from Olaf who would use Igor's weaknesses against him.

His great-great grandfather's viola rested in its case in the corner. Igor hadn't played it in weeks. To play meant to remember. For some reason, he wanted to remember now.

He unlatched the case and took out the instrument. He ran his fingers over strings and wood, feeling as though he were greeting an old friend. He called it a stream of Russian endearments. He let the cold place in his heart thaw for just a moment. Then he forced himself to erect another wall, freeze it again, become his father's son instead of his mother's. Because he couldn't be both. And being his mother's son might get him killed.

Chapter 2

"New shipment is coming in tonight," Olaf stated.

"Another one?" Igor asked. "That makes three this week."

Olaf stretched out his long legs, the towel around his waist secure. They were grown men conducting a business meeting in a sauna. It was there *territorya*—territory. They owned the bathhouse.

Olaf's brown gaze narrowed when he looked at Igor. A flash of disdain blasted through his eyes and then mellowed into disappointment.

"You will be there."

"Da. Yes."

He nodded once. "Good. Good. The men need to see you there. As my heir, they need to know you will rule with an iron fist."

Igor said nothing.

"You should see one of the girls," Olaf commented. "Maybe that will do something for your attitude."

Igor's attitude would change when the meeting ended. "I don't need a woman."

"No?"

Igor smiled, showing an excess amount of teeth. "I need several."

Olaf laughed and slapped his knee. "Maybe you are my son after all." He looked at Igor to see how he'd taken that statement.

Igor learned long ago not to show emotion.

"I think several women is a good idea." Olaf stood, adjusted his towel, and sauntered to the door. "Petrovich!" he barked.

"Sir?" The blond man who had been silent during their meeting, shifted on the raised platform behind Igor.

"Make sure my son doesn't get himself killed tonight."

"I'll do my best, sir."

Olaf nodded and then left the sauna. The heavy door closed, and the tension dissipated immediately.

"That went well," Sasha Petrovich stated, moving from behind Igor to sit next to him.

"I suppose. He's getting relentless."

"About making sure you're involved in every aspect of the business, you mean?"

"Among other things," Igor muttered. "There's something up his sleeve. He just won't tell me what it is."

"What's going on with you?" Sasha asked.

"What do you mean?"

He sighed. "How long have we known each other?"

"Too long."

"How long, Igor?"

"Since we were seven."

"Yes. I'm your best friend, your right-hand man, and your bodyguard. I'm the only one who knows how you truly feel about your father."

"Not true," Igor interjected. "My father knows."

They fell silent and Igor looked at his lap. How did he

admit to his oldest friend that he was tired and numb, that the endless parade of women and the life of organized crime were eating away at him? How he still felt haunted by his mother's hopes and dreams for him. How he warred with himself about touching the viola lest it bring about a surge of emotion and endless pain he couldn't control.

Control was all Igor had.

"I feel old," Igor admitted.

"You're only twenty-nine."

"Old is old. I want something else. But I don't know what."

"Let me buy you a drink."

"I don't want a drink," he growled. The steam of the sauna curled around them. Igor breathed it in, feeling the hot, sweaty air stick to him. "Go."

"I'm not leaving you. Not in this mental state."

Igor didn't smile at Sasha's good humor. "How does this life not affect you?"

Sasha shrugged. "I made my peace with it. You haven't. Until you do, you'll feel pulled in two different directions."

"Thank you for the diagnosis," Igor replied dryly.

"My pleasure. Sure you don't want to get a drink?"

Igor shook his head. "You go. I'm going to sit here for a minute."

Sasha got up from his seat and looked at the man he called best friend. With one final nod, he left. Igor leaned his head back against the wall and closed his eyes. The door opened and Igor sighed.

"Sasha, I swear, I'm fine."

A light, feminine chuckle tickled his ears.

Igor's eyes flew open, but he didn't move. Couldn't. The woman's piercing blue gaze froze him to his seat.

"Sorry to disappoint you," she said, laughing at him in silent humor.

Igor's gaze meandered down her body. A lean, slender form was covered in a tasteful one piece. "Not at all disappointed."

Her easy smile slipped. Nervousness permeated the air, and she shifted her stance, no doubt wanting to bolt. "Listen, I just want to sit in the sauna and relax, okay? I'm not here to get hit on or to make idle chit-chat."

"You're welcome to go to another sauna. The spa has four," Igor replied. He hoped she didn't leave, but he wasn't about to beg a woman to stay. No matter how attractive. Her dark blond hair was pulled up into a messy ponytail, the heat and steam of the sauna curling the tendrils at her temples and nape.

She glared. "They're occupied. One is a loud, drunken bachelorette party. Another is a couple doing…things. Another is a group of men."

"Sit down. I won't bother you."

The young woman paused for just a moment before deciding she could take him at his word. She set her white towel down on the bench, the farthest one away from him, and stretched out her legs.

Leaning back, she closed her eyes and her breath steadied.

Igor had given women apathy a time or two. He couldn't say he cared to be on the receiving end of it—especially from this woman. There was something about her. Like it took all of her effort to stay still when she'd rather be moving, dancing, experiencing.

"What's your name?" Igor asked.

Without opening her eyes, she replied, "You said you wouldn't bother me."

"I'm just asking your name."

"And after I give you my name, are you going to want my phone number, too?"

A chuckle escaped his mouth. He couldn't have been more surprised. It was a rarity for him to be taken so off guard. "Damn, you're arrogant."

"And you're not?" she shot back.

"Why would you think I'm arrogant?" Igor held in a smile. The woman either didn't know who he was or didn't care, but she was talking to him.

"Look at you," she stated.

"Look at me, what?"

"Are you really going to make me say it?"

"You don't want to talk to me because I'm good-looking?" Igor asked.

Her nostrils flared in annoyance. He found it endearing.

"No, I don't want to talk to you because I'm here to have a steam and that's it."

"But you do find me good-looking," he pressed, needing—wanting—to prove something. To her or himself, he didn't know. When she continued to glare, he went on, "Adorable? Handsome? Sinfully sexy? Ah, I see you're about to smile. Might as well give in."

The corners of her lips twitched, slowly pulling into a bright grin. It changed everything about her. Turned her from cute to irresistible.

"Is this your usual MO? Bug women into talking to you?" she asked lightly.

"When it works, it works, no?"

"Where are you from?"

"New York—Sheepshead Bay."

"Ah. Explains the thick accent."

"Thick accent? I don't have a thick accent."

"Okay."

"I don't."

"Hate to break it to you, sport, but yeah, ya do." She looked at him in confusion. "What's wrong with having an accent? I'd kill for an accent. I'd love to be exotic."

"You don't need an accent for that."

"So, what, you're not proud of your roots?"

"I thought you wanted to sit in silence."

"Oh, I've gotten under your skin, hmmm? Tell me why you don't like your accent, and I'll tell you my name."

The air in the room swelled and seemed to grow hotter. No matter how much he may have wanted her, lust wasn't built for confession.

"Not a fair trade. But if you're here the same time, same day next week, I might consider telling you."

Chapter 3

A month after Igor's mother died, he got his nose broken for the first time by a big, stupid oaf of a boy who lacked basic human compassion. Smaller than other children his age, Igor preferred reading to sports and playing the viola to socializing with his peers. He was an anomaly and a natural target.

His father called him weak.

John Patrick caught Igor one afternoon as St. Joseph's let out. Children in uniforms blasted the doors open, eager to escape the strict confines and parameters of their education. Igor had stayed behind to ask a question about homework and to receive just a bit of motherly affection from the young nun who had a soft spot for the motherless child.

As Igor shoved his belongings into his backpack, he didn't pay attention to the empty halls or the fact that John Patrick was waiting for him. The bully shoved him, and Igor stepped on his own untied shoelaces and tumbled to the floor, his half open bag spilling pens, pencils, and other school supplies.

John Patrick grabbed Igor by the collar and hauled him

close. An ugly sneer marred his face as he dragged Igor to the side exit, out into the unknown.

"I hate you," the bully yelled.

Why? Igor wanted to ask, but there was no point since there was a fist colliding with his nose. Cartilage crunched and blood oozed. The thug laughed and laughed, and even though Igor was already down, the kid kicked him in the ribs before spitting on the ground and leaving.

After a time, Igor managed to pick himself up but not before he threw up the contents of his stomach. He hobbled and wobbled home. His father didn't think to send a car to and from school for his only son, a boy who had already proven he wasn't as physically strong as others.

When Igor walked into his house—it had ceased being home the moment his mother passed—his father was waiting for him. Olaf took in Igor's bloodied skin, his bruised eyes, the puke on his shirt, and barked out questions in Russian.

Igor answered dispassionately in the same tongue.

"You're a disgrace," his father spat. "Be a man. Fight back." He whirled from the room, leaving his son to clean himself up.

The housekeeper, a plump gray-haired woman who had been eavesdropping at the kitchen door, finally came into the room. Igor waved her away and insisted he was old enough to take care of himself.

That night, he didn't sleep. He plotted, thinking about how to destroy the bully's life. Igor did not have brute strength, but as his mother had so often reminded him when she was alive, he had a brilliant mind—and he used it now.

At school the next day, the kids whispered behind their hands but didn't dare ask him what had transpired. The bully snickered in the corner of the classroom. Igor stared at him with unflinching brown eyes.

John Patrick's smile slipped.

Sister Margaret, a middle-aged nun with no tolerance for shenanigans, held Igor after class and demanded to know what had happened to him.

Igor feigned embarrassment when he mumbled, "Nothing."

"Igor," Sister Margaret began, her face lined with a frown. "Your eyes are black, and your nose is clearly broken. Something happened to you. Tell me."

"I tripped," he lied.

"Your father, did he—"

"No," Igor hastened to assure her. He bit his lip and looked at his lap. "It was a student."

"What happened?" she tried again, somehow managing to soften her voice.

"I was using the bathroom …" Igor said quietly, so quietly that Sister Margaret had to lean closer to hear him.

"Go on."

"John Patrick came in and he—" Igor looked up from his lap. "He tried to kiss me. When I told him no, and that it's a sin, he became violent and angry. He punched me in the nose." Igor stood up and lifted his shirt to show her the bruises along his ribs. "He did this, too." He dropped his shirt and sat back down.

"Thank you, Igor. You may go," Sister Margaret dismissed.

The next day, John Patrick was noticeably absent from school. It only took Igor one whisper alluding to what hadn't happened for the entire school to believe it to be true. That whisper followed John Patrick through high school, causing far more damage than a broken nose.

Chapter 4

That night, Igor, with Sasha as his right hand, went to the docks to check the incoming shipment. It was light. Igor didn't care why or how. Sasha and Igor took the man who tried to fleece them to an empty warehouse and tortured him for hours.

It was barely dawn when he made it back to his apartment. He was covered in blood—none of it his. After stripping in the foyer, Igor bagged up his soiled clothes and set them aside to be thrown out. Naked, he strolled to the liquor cart and poured himself a glass of vodka. It wasn't the cheap stuff, nor was it the high end. Somewhere in between.

That's how he felt himself.

The first time Igor had killed a man, he'd thrown up. He threw up every time since, but he soon learned that a woman—or several—helped him forget. After the women came the vodka. He drank himself into a drunken stupor and then vomited up vodka and bile.

Not even Sasha knew how he reconciled his actions.

He hated his father—for many reasons—and yet somehow, he couldn't find a way to get out from under Olaf's thumb. He wasn't sure he wanted to. Igor harbored secret hopes that one day his father would be proud of his son and heir.

He looked at the clock. He had a few hours to shower and look presentable before sitting aside his father at church. Every Sunday, father and son would attend mass, sit in their separate confessionals, and then they'd have lunch at a Russian restaurant around the corner.

Igor sat in the confessional every week and refused to say a word to the priest. After fifteen minutes of silence, Father Michael would give Igor ten Hail Marys and call it a day. Igor didn't believe in confession, but he did believe in facades.

"You look like hell," Olaf stated in way of greeting when they arrived on the steps of St. Nicholas Cathedral.

Igor raised an eyebrow but said nothing. He hadn't slept in thirty-six hours, and all he had in his system was coffee and vodka.

After confession, they walked to the tiny Russian restaurant that was just one of Olaf's many money-laundering fronts. "The Drugovs are in town," Olaf said after they were served their borscht.

"How nice."

"They are bringing their daughter."

Though his senses were sluggish, Igor's warning bells went off. "Daughter," he repeated flatly.

"You remember Katarina?"

"*Da.*"

"You will take her to the opera on Friday night."

"Will I?" Igor asked quietly.

"The Drugovs are wealthy and powerful."

"I'm aware," Igor said.

"She's beautiful."

"There are plenty of beautiful women I could spend my time with," Igor pointed out.

"But you will marry only one."

And there it was. Olaf wanted to expand his empire—to do that he needed the Drugovs. His son wasn't enough. Never would be.

The borscht turned bitter in his mouth, but he forced himself to keep eating as if Olaf hadn't told him what his future looked like.

"Say something," Olaf snapped.

"What would you have me say?" Igor asked in genuine curiosity. "You clearly think to move me like a piece on a chessboard."

"You are my heir and successor. I'm thinking of my legacy."

"Ah, yes, your precious legacy."

"I could end you," Olaf blustered.

"You could. But then who would run your empire?" He pushed back from the table and stood. "If you'll excuse me."

"So polite," Olaf mocked. "Even when you wish to kill me. You *are* your mother's son."

Igor smiled and gave a scornful bow. "Thank you."

Without looking back, Igor walked out on his father.

After walking out on his father, Igor called Sasha.

The two friends sat in one of their favorite bars, a small dive around the corner from the Russian bathhouse where they did business. It was dark, empty, and quiet. The bartender knew them and knew to ignore them.

"So are you going to marry her?" Sasha asked.

"I don't know," Igor admitted, swirling the clear liquid in his glass.

"What do you gain by marrying her?" Sasha prodded. "Versus what you lose by not."

"Could I have a different life?" Igor wondered aloud. "Go somewhere far away and not be my father's son?"

"Why do care so much about it? What hold does he have on you aside from blood?"

Igor didn't answer and took a drink.

"There is another option," Sasha said.

"No."

Sasha shrugged.

"You would do it, wouldn't you? If I said 'yes'," Igor pressed.

"I follow you—not him."

Sasha's unwavering loyalty humbled Igor to the core.

"I've met her before. She isn't a complete stranger," Igor admitted.

"And?"

"We were teenagers the last time we saw each other."

"I'm waiting."

Despite the situation, Igor smiled. "She took my virginity."

"No shit," Sasha said with a laugh.

Igor had been fifteen, quiet, and studious. Katarina, only a year older, was vibrant and gorgeous. She and her family had come to stay at the Dolinsky country home in Pennsylvania. One night, she'd snuck into his bedroom, draped her naked body on top of his, and turned him from boy to man. It had only taken about thirty seconds. She'd visited his room every night for two weeks until she and her parents had left.

"Damn, how did I not know about this?" Sasha asked.

"That was the summer that you—"

"*Da.* I remember," Sasha interrupted.

They were silent a moment, both thinking about that summer for different reasons. Unable to help himself, Igor wondered how it would be between him and Katarina now, as adults.

He sighed. "I guess I'll take her to the opera."

Chapter 5

Katarina Drugov was haughty. Haughty and gorgeous—and the woman knew it. She kept Igor waiting until five minutes before the curtain rose before gracing him with her presence.

Gone was the sexually forward teenage girl, and in her place was a woman he wanted to break.

He ignored her through the first act of *La Traviata,* and during the intermission, he refused to introduce her to the friends and colleagues that paid their respects at their private box.

Katarina must have hated being disregarded because she appeared to do everything she could to entice Igor. A brush of her hand here, a calculated look there. But he pretended he didn't notice.

During the second act, she grew bold, letting her fingers wander across his tuxedo pants. She slowly undid the zipper and let her hand inside.

He wasn't wearing underwear.

His erection swelled in her hand, and still he didn't take his attention off the performance. He leaned back in his chair, stretched out his long legs, and pointedly looked at her. They had a silent battle of wills.

She removed her hand and got on her knees.

Igor didn't touch her, and even when he filled her mouth with his essence, he didn't move from his position—not even to help her back to her chair.

Katarina gracefully rose from her position on the ground and discreetly wiped her lips. Returning to her seat, she kept her eyes trained on him for the rest of the final act. It was only when the curtain closed, and everyone stood to applaud that Igor looked at her and spoke.

"I found the performance completely satisfactory."

"They want us to get married," Igor said to Katarina that night when they were in his bed.

She stretched her long legs and then curled her body against his, letting her fingers linger on his chest. The delicate platinum band she wore on her middle finger shone in the low lamplight. "Would that be so terrible?"

Her long, black hair spilled across his arm as he shifted. "You don't have a problem with your parents dictating your life?"

"Who said anything about dictating?"

Igor looked at her. The lamplight bathed her skin in a soft, warm glow. She was beautiful. And cold. "You want this."

"*Da.*"

"Why?" he pressed. "You don't love me."

She laughed in genuine amusement. "Since when does marriage have anything to do with love?"

Brittle disappointment settled into his bones. He wasn't naive, or even a dreamer. And though his parents' marriage had been nothing he wanted to mirror, they had once loved each other. In their own broken way.

"Oh, you were hoping for that, weren't you?" She turned her laughter onto him. It was ugly and mocking, and he refused to let her get away with it. He grasped her arms and rolled on top of her.

Her eyes widened in fear and then pleasure as he took her mouth in a punishing kiss. He hated her in that moment, hated everything she represented and everything about himself he was unable to purge.

In the morning, they both walked away sated, bruised, and with an understanding. They were going to let their parents think they were mulling over marriage—and in the meantime, everyone would get what they wanted. Olaf would expand his empire and the Drugovs would gain a stronghold in the United States.

Igor opened the town car door for Katarina and smiled down at her. It was all mockery. "Until next time, my love."

She gave him a lingering kiss on the lips. In his ear, she whispered, "Think of my tongue. Doing delicious things to you."

He wished he could say her words didn't turn him on, but he was a man, and he enjoyed her body.

"Think of mine, Katarina. The next time we're together, I won't let you come for hours."

He watched his words penetrate, and she shivered in anticipation.

Who needed love when there was lust?

His body hurt. Katarina had been a worthy bed partner. He recognized her for what she was: a chameleon, a woman who became whatever any man wanted her to be.

If he'd wanted to make love to her, she would've moaned and accepted it. But they didn't love, they fucked.

Igor went to the Russian bathhouse for a steam and contemplation. He walked that fine line of wanting to please his father and wanting to defy him. Deep down, he was still the hurt little boy who'd lost his mother, wanting nothing more than his father's love and attention.

The sauna was empty save for him, and he hoped it remained that way. Closing his eyes, he slipped into a doze, jarring awake when the door opened. He silently cursed in Russian but ceased immediately when he saw the intruder.

He smiled. "You came back."

Tossing long, blond hair up into a quick, messy bun, she replied, "I didn't come for you, I came for the steam."

"Right."

She rolled her eyes and settled her towel on the opposite side of the room and sat down. Her bathing suit was another tasteful one piece, concealing attributes that most women seemed to flaunt.

"You're staring," she pointed out with a small smile.

A slight grin appeared on his lips. "No. I'm examining. There's a difference."

"Examining?"

"Yes."

She shrugged.

"Do you live in the neighborhood?" he asked.

Pausing for a moment, she relented and shook her head.

"What's your name?" he asked.

"Why do you hate your accent?" she fired back.

"Round and round we go."

"Seems like it."

There was something about this woman. She went head to head with him, wasn't intimidated by him, didn't know who he was, so she didn't know what he could offer her. He suddenly found he liked that. When talking with her, he didn't have to be his father's disappointment.

Maybe if he offered her something of true value, she'd reveal in kind.

"I don't hate my accent," he said. "But it reminds me of my history—a history I'd rather not talk about." He wasn't proud of his past, or his present. The future was still unwritten, but the way his life was going, he didn't think he was going to be proud of that either.

"Roots are roots. Dig them up and you die."

He raised his eyebrows. "And your roots?"

"Swedish." She traced a finger along the wooden bench. "You don't have to be anything you don't want to be."

"That's a bit naive, don't you think?"

"Maybe. I prefer hopeful."

"You just spoke of digging up your roots."

"No. I was just making a point. Look, there are all things in all our pasts we don't like or wish we could change. But then we wouldn't be who we are—where we are."

He smiled in rancor. "You like who you are, then? Because a lot of us don't."

"So change."

Igor let out a laugh. "Change? Just like that?"

"Sure, why not?"

"It's not as easy as all that."

"Well, of course not. Nothing worthwhile ever is."

His brow furrowed as he contemplated her. "What did you change in your life?"

"Everything."

She spoke lightly, but he detected something deeper,

something she was concealing. He wanted to know what it was.

"Did you change things? Or did change happen to you?" he wondered aloud.

"A little bit of both, I think."

Igor knew a bit about that.

"How old are you?" he asked.

"How old are you?"

It was on the tip of his tongue to ask if she knew who he was, but then he thought better of it. He didn't think she'd appreciate the arrogance, and it might do more harm than good. The last thing he wanted her to do was disappear on him—she invigorated him, helped clear his mind —better than a good steam.

Something about her made him want to pretend to be unassuming. Maybe he could be himself with her. Whoever that was.

"I'm twenty-nine," he answered.

She raised an eyebrow. "You look older."

"If I said that to a woman, I'd have to worry about assault."

"True." She chuckled. "But then again, men seem to carry years better. But you look… I don't know…hard."

"I am hard," he admitted blithely. "Now it's your turn. How are old are you?"

"Twenty-four."

"Young."

"Don't do that," she snapped, glaring.

"Do what?"

"Don't assume that because I'm young I'm an idiot."

"When did I give the impression that I thought you were an idiot?" he asked calmly, enjoying her fire.

"You old people always assume that," she grumbled.

Igor laughed. "Would you like to go out for drinks?"

"I never go out just for drinks. If a man's serious, he'll offer to take me to dinner."

"I'd offer to take you to dinner," he said, not missing a beat, "but I don't know your name."

Cocking her head to the side, she paused, considering. "Mary. My name is Mary."

"Mary, would you like to go to dinner with me?"

She smiled as she said, "No."

Chapter 6

Igor was twenty years old when he killed his first man. He'd looked the traitor in the face before blowing his head clean off.

It was the only time Igor could remember Olaf looking at him with anything resembling pride.

After disposing of the body, Igor had showered and puked in the tub. Then he got stinking drunk, puked again, and then passed out. As the sun had risen and shone through the open curtains, causing Igor to wake and wince, he realized he couldn't stay soft if he had any hope of surviving in his father's world. He packed up his viola, put on a custom-made suit, and became his father's successor.

He hated every moment of it. The meetings, the petty squabbles, the shifty eyes everyone gave everyone else. He constantly had to watch his back. Sasha had volunteered to watch it for him.

"You don't want into this life," Igor protested. "Trust me."

"We're friends. Best friends. If it weren't for you..." he trailed off. "I can help you."

"How?"

With Sasha's aid, Igor had gone from scrawny and soft, to cut and lethal. They practiced schooling their features, knowing there would be a time when they couldn't react, no matter what terrible things they'd see. They caroused and drank, seduced women, indulged like men who knew life was fleeting. Sasha taught Igor how to live and planted the idea that Igor should overthrow his father—sooner rather than later.

"Not the time," Igor always said.

"Well, when?" Sasha demanded. "We're ready to follow you."

"I know. Just—I know." He wasn't ready. To end Olaf's reign, his son would have to kill him. There would be no going back, no pretending he wasn't already damned to the devil. Somehow, he could rationalize the embezzling, the laundering, the murders of traitors and opponents. But to contemplate patricide, and then plan it and execute it… He was familiar with Shakespeare's tragedies.

Sasha sighed but let it go. Igor never did anything until he was good and ready. He'd take Sasha's advice into consideration but make his own choice.

The years of tenuous prosperity continued. Igor recognized the changing world and knew something had to be done. He wanted to expand into different sectors, focus on utilizing technology instead of city contracts. Olaf wouldn't hear of it. Steadfast in his convictions, he continued to run things as he always had.

It was then that Igor realized his father had no vision. If they wanted to remain powerful, they would have to change the way they operated. So Igor was stuck in a world he didn't want to be in, all the while trying to figure out how to change it without resorting to more violence.

He continued to live in limbo, but it was only recently

that he had begun to feel like he'd been shoved into a pressure cooker. The lid was ready to blow. Meeting Mary at the Russian bathhouse had been like releasing the steam valve. He instantly felt soothed, the tension inside of him easing. Though she was young in age, she carried herself like a woman who knew her identity. She had no tolerance for bullshit. She was attractive and her assets were clearly presented, but she didn't flaunt—nor did she hide.

And she was completely resistant to him. They spoke and laughed and engaged and even though they had a tacit agreement to meet every Saturday at the same time, she never accepted more from him. Not a ride home nor his invitations to dinner. He couldn't figure her out. A lesser man would've been annoyed and given up, but he enjoyed the intellectual chase. Igor wanted her, originally for her body. Now, he wanted her because she soothed the hatred and violence burning him up from the inside.

It had been a month since they'd met, and he was no closer to wearing her down. "Why won't you go out to dinner with me?" he finally asked as they walked out of the bathhouse.

She wrapped a plaid scarf around her neck before burrowing into her thick bubble coat. It was only forty degrees, and she looked dressed for winter in Siberia. "Because."

"That's not an answer," he growled.

She stared at him with guileless blue eyes. "Truth?"

"Please. I can handle it."

"I don't have time for distractions." When he was about to scoff at her excuse, she interrupted, "Seriously. I really don't have time for distractions—and you'd be the biggest distraction ever."

"What's taking up all of your time? College?"

"No."

"Work?"

"No."

"Personal."

She paused. "Yes." Mary didn't say more about it. "Will you please take my word for it? I do like you, Igor. If things were different, I'd go to dinner with you. I'd go to a lot of dinners with you." When she admitted the truth, she stared him in the eye.

His hands reached out to gently grasp her arms and pull her towards him.

"Don't," she pleaded, her gloved hands coming up to rest on his chest.

He gave her the chance to pull away, but when she didn't and looked up at him with wide, innocent eyes, he dipped his head and kissed her. Igor didn't hold back—he wanted this woman, in a way he had never wanted anything. Instead of taking what he wanted, he gave. Gave her everything that he was. And before he knew it, she was kissing him back, holding onto him for dear life.

Part of him knew he shouldn't be kissing Mary in front of the Russian bathhouse. Anyone could see and tell Olaf what his son was up to.

With great resolve, he lifted his mouth from hers. Her eyes remained closed, her lips pouty and rosy from his kiss. He wanted nothing more than to bury his hands in her hair and pull her to him again and lose himself in her.

"Have dinner with me," he urged.

She slowly opened her eyes. They were sad and solemn. "No."

Chapter 7

He walked home in the winter rain, not caring about the cold or that the wetness seeped into his clothes. He welcomed the idea of contracting pneumonia. Maybe then his chest wouldn't feel so empty.

What was it about her?

Was it just the fact that she was elusive? Or was it something more? He loved talking to her. For the first time in years, he didn't have to guard his words, and aside from the fact that she refused to reveal anything about her personal life, she spoke with a forthright honesty that called him on his shit.

He needed that.

She was strong and beautiful and intelligent. He was a man who knew what he wanted, and what he wanted was her. But he didn't have the slightest clue how to *win* her.

The next morning, as he sat next to his father in church holding in his sneezes, he prayed to the Virgin for guidance. He didn't know if she was listening, but he hoped like hell she heard his plea and took pity on him.

The Virgin must've been deaf that day. Mary didn't

show up at the bathhouse the next weekend. Had he scared her off? Was she finally done with whatever they were?

Sitting in the sauna, he placed his head in his hands. The door opened and he looked up with raptured hope on his face, only to be completely disappointed when he saw it was Sasha.

Igor couldn't hold in a Russian curse.

"Good to see you too," Sasha drawled before taking a seat next to him. "What's with you? You've been in a mood all week."

Igor hesitated. Though Sasha was his best friend and confidant, he still wasn't sure if he wanted to explain he was tied up in knots over a woman—a woman who'd refused to give him her last name, refused to give him her cell phone number, refused his dinner invitations, refused...*him.*

"Ah," Sasha said, not taking his ice blue eyes off Igor.

"'Ah' what?" Igor growled.

Sasha grinned. "Who is she?"

He debated all of five seconds before coming clean. "Mary."

"As in Virgin?"

"Shut up."

Sasha laughed. "Tell me more."

Igor explained how they'd met and been meeting every Saturday for the last month in the sauna.

"And she didn't show up yet?" Sasha asked. "Day's not over."

"She's not coming," Igor lamented bleakly.

"You don't know that."

Igor rubbed a hand across his face.

"Are you worried about her?"

"No. I—last week we didn't—I kissed her and asked her to dinner. She turned me down."

"She must be insane. What woman would say no to you?"

Igor smiled without humor. "I'm touched by your loyalty. Mary doesn't know my last name—and all that comes with it."

"Why not?"

"Because she's not the kind of woman that would be impressed by it."

"Right," Sasha scoffed. "Because women are rarely attracted to wealthy, handsome men."

"How did I build that wealth?" Igor reminded him.

"She might surprise you," Sasha said, ignoring Igor's pointed question about the life they led. "Don't make decisions for her just because you're afraid to show her your true self."

Igor's fist shot out and connected with Sasha's jaw. Sasha returned in kind. They wailed on each other, two grown men in swimsuits, decking it out in a sauna. When they'd finally exhausted themselves, they reclaimed their seats and pretended as though nothing had occurred.

"You're acting like a victim," Sasha said, gingerly touching his split lip. His finger came away bloody. "When you should be doing everything you can to find this girl."

"We didn't exchange phone numbers and last names for a reason."

"I've never seen you this way over a woman."

Igor said nothing.

"You do remember you own this establishment."

"*Da*," Igor said in understanding. He had access to security footage and account information. Those that used the facilities either had a membership or were given a guest pass. Either way, names and phone numbers were accounted for.

"Not a word of this to anyone," Igor warned, rising.

"Iron vault," Sasha assured him.

The writing was on the wall—he was acting like a lovesick lunatic, and he wasn't going to do a damn thing to stop it.

∽

Igor stood on the porch of a Long Island home, wondering if he'd made a mistake. The unassuming, modest Mary couldn't possibly live here. *Here* was a gargantuan house that bordered on monstrosity. A light dusting of snow covered the lawns, the pruned and bare trees looked silver in the weak, winter sunlight.

He raised his hand to press the doorbell button but hesitated. What would she do if she saw him? Would she throw him off her property? How did a twenty-four-old woman have this kind of wealth? Unless it was family money.

Wanting answers finally overrode his worries. He pressed the doorbell and waited. The winter chill teased the back of his neck, but he refused to pull up the collar of his coat, not wanting to look like he was fidgeting.

The door opened, revealing a man with dark hair, a thin, wiry body, and a puzzled look. "May I help you?" he asked in heavily accented English. Igor couldn't place the country of origin.

"I think I have the wrong house," Igor murmured, staring into the man's steady green eyes. Igor turned to leave when he heard her voice.

"Auggie? Who is it?"

"I don't know yet, *múzám*," the man named Auggie said, his eyes remaining on Igor.

He saw her blond head and that damn messy top bun that he loved so much. And then she was peeking out from behind the man's side, her hand lingering on his waist. Her touch was intimate, familiar, rightful.

She never touched him that way.

Igor swallowed.

"Igor," she exclaimed in genuine surprise.

"Ah, he's a friend of yours." Auggie smiled and stepped back. "Please, please. Come in."

Bemused, Igor stepped through the doorway into the foyer. If he'd been paying more attention to the decor, he would've appreciated the rich and warm interior, the colorful walls, bright paintings, and comfortable furniture. But he wasn't paying enough attention—his sole focus was on the woman. She wore a long, green silk robe that hugged her curves yet revealed no skin. That was her— modest vixen.

She was driving him insane.

"I would've called but I..." Igor trailed off. What could he really say?

"It's fine," she said distractedly.

The three of them headed into the expansive kitchen. High-end appliances graced the marble countertops, the white cabinets custom-made.

"Maybe your friend would like something to drink?" Auggie suggested to her.

She nodded. "Yes." She looked at Igor. "Something to drink?"

"Water, if you please."

After filling a glass with ice and water from the refrigerator, she handed it to him. He clutched it and forced himself to take a sip even though he wasn't thirsty.

Auggie touched Mary's cheek, whispered something in a foreign language, and then briefly kissed her on the lips. "Please excuse me," Auggie said to Igor. "I'm in the middle of something and it cannot wait." Igor nodded even as Auggie strode purposefully from the room.

The air crackled with tension as Igor stared at her, willing the pieces of the puzzle to fall into place and make sense to him.

She fingered a delicate gold chain at her neck, looking at a spot on the counter.

"So," Igor said, his voice breaking the silence. "Who the hell are you and why have you lied to me?"

Chapter 8

Igor's question lingered in the air.

"I've never lied to you," she said after a time.

"You said your name was Mary."

She rolled her eyes. "My name *is* Mary. Maryruth. You've never heard of a nickname?"

"You said you didn't have time for distractions because of something personal. *That*—" he pointed in the direction of Auggie, "is more than personal."

She tapped her long, elegant fingers on the marble. They faced each other, the countertop between them.

"Maryruth suits you," he said quietly.

"How did you find me?" she asked.

"I know the owner of the bathhouse. Got your contact information that way."

"Ah," she said, not looking like she particularly cared one way or the other about the invasion of privacy. "Why are you here?"

"You're not glad to see me?" When she remained stoic, he replied, "I waited for you—on Saturday. You never showed. I was worried."

"Were you?"

"I had to see you."

There. He admitted it. And he didn't care that it made him sound weak or that he was bending. He wanted to flex because the moment he became completely unyielding was the day he turned into his father.

"I wasn't avoiding you," she said slowly. "I promise. Auggie had…a crisis."

"Is he," Igor swallowed, "your lover?"

"Yes," she admitted easily.

A bomb went off in his head.

"I was named for my grandmother," she said, changing the subject. "Maryruth Baldwin. Made the best damn strawberry rhubarb pie in all of Iowa. She had blue ribbons from the state fair to prove it."

"What does that have to do with—"

She raised her blond brows. "I'm getting to it. You want the scoop?" When he reluctantly nodded, she went on, "I was born in Iowa and didn't want to die in Iowa. When I was eighteen, I packed up a suitcase and came to New York."

"You came to New York with nothing?"

"Not nothing. I'd managed to save a little bit of money—birthday money, Christmas money. I worked when I was in high school. Waitress at a local haunt."

He nodded.

"So I got to New York, found a cheap room in an apartment with a nice girl. Wasn't the safest place to live, but it was clean, and she took me under her wing. Got me a job at her restaurant. Tiny little place in the West Village.

"It was a Friday night. Place was packed. Auggie walked in and sat alone at the bar. He was quiet, respectful. He asked for a glass of red of my choosing." She took a breath. "It felt important, you know? Like it was a test. I gave him something soft and soothing. Warm. That's how he described it anyway."

She smiled and shook her head.

Igor was lost in her story, letting her lead him down the windy trail of memories. She'd tell him, when she was ready. Always when she was ready.

"He introduced himself. Agoston Boros."

Igor frowned. The name seemed familiar, but he couldn't place it.

"I had no idea who he was," she admitted, "Until another waitress told me he was a well-known Hungarian painter. She said he came in all the time and would leave sketches on the back of menus. One was framed and signed in the manager's office.

"Auggie paid, tipped well—but not too well—and left. He came back the next night. And the night after that. And so on. Finally, after about a week of this, he stayed while I closed the restaurant. The manager was downstairs counting money and Auggie hadn't moved from his bar stool.

"*You know who I am*, he said. I told him I did. He asked if I'd like to see his paintings. I told him yes. The next day he took me to the MOMA to see them. They were paintings from over a decade ago—Auggie hadn't had a showing of anything new in that long. He'd been painting, but he wasn't happy or satisfied with anything he was creating.

"The night we met at the restaurant, he went home and painted until dawn. He painted *me*, Igor. He called me his muse and said he needed me. He offered me the world. And I took it."

She fell silent and waited.

"He's got to be, what? Twice your age? Was sleeping with him part of the deal?" he asked.

Half of her mouth quirked up into a smile. "Did you just ask me if I was a whore?"

He flinched as though she'd slapped him. His eyes dropped in shame.

"Not that it matters, but he's only about twenty years older than me, okay? And it wasn't part of the deal. But when a man paints you in the nude, down to the freckles on your knees, you feel *seen*. In a way you've never been seen before. I gave myself to him, Igor. And he was grateful for it. Honored. So was I.

"Maybe it's narcissistic, but Auggie needs me. He needs me to create the one thing that drives his soul. How could I not share my body with him on the most basic of levels?"

"You love him," he said quietly.

"Of course. But Igor. There are different types of love."

How was it this young woman was schooling him—*him*—a man of his position and power and knowledge? He felt like a fool.

"You're not what you seem, you know. You made me think you were young and naive."

"I made you think no such thing," she scoffed. "I warned you, didn't I? I told you not to make assumptions because of my age."

She shook her head in disappointment. "I don't talk to my parents. Well, I should say they don't talk to me. They don't understand. They're deeply religious and conservative and they see everything in black and white, right and wrong. I've made my peace with that." She swallowed.

He stared at her for a very long time, memorizing the curve of her shoulder, the outline of her ear. He finally understood the robe she wore—she was an artist's subject. A muse.

He couldn't compete with that. He had nothing to give her but a dangerous life. And his heart.

Why would she choose a man's love when she could inspire another man's greatness?

Chapter 9

He didn't see Maryruth again. She stopped coming to the Russian bathhouse. Whenever he thought of her, he thought of her as Maryruth. 'Mary' hadn't done her justice. It was as if she needed two names to tell the world of her vibrancy, her passion, her clarity.

Damn it all to hell. He felt like a teenager who'd had his heart broken for the first time. Though he wasn't a teenager, there was truth to the statement. Until Maryruth, he'd never been in love before. His heart had been broken when his mother died because she'd left him.

Maryruth had left him.

No, that wasn't really true. She'd never been with him in the first place, so how could she leave him? Still, he felt abandoned.

Night after night, as the winter snow turned to early spring rain, he drank. He drank but couldn't get her out of his head. Sasha told him he was spiraling. His father berated him for his lack of focus.

He didn't care about any of it.

Katarina came into town, but he made up an excuse

not to see her. In true Russian fashion, he was good at wallowing in his vodka.

One particularly terrible, wet, and dark Tuesday after a business meeting gone wrong, he went home and tried to shower off the day. Just as he was wrapping a towel around his waist, the apartment phone rang.

"Mr. Dolinsky," the doorman said.

"Charlie, what can I do for you?" Igor asked. Droplets of water dusted his skin, his wet, brown hair falling into his eyes.

"You have a visitor. She says her name is Maryruth."

His heart nearly dropped out of his chest. "Send her up." Blood rushed through his veins as he stumbled to his room to throw on a quick change of clothes. He didn't bother looking to see if they matched. Holding his breath, he waited for the knock.

It was tentative, indecisive. So unlike Maryruth.

He opened the door and stared. She stood on his threshold, drenched, blond hair plastered to her neck. Rainwater dribbled down her cheeks, or…were those tears?

Without a word, he grasped her arm and hauled her inside his apartment and against his chest. He held her to him as she cried, her entire body a shaking force. He whispered words in Russian against her wet hair, reveling that she was in his apartment. Igor didn't care why she was there or that she was an emotional mess. He was glad and for the first time in weeks, his heart was lighter.

When her sobs quieted, she finally pulled back. "Sorry," she muttered in embarrassment, mopping at her tears.

"Don't be sorry," he said gruffly. Taking her by the hand, he led her farther into his apartment, not caring that her shoes were tracking mud onto the wood floors.

He brought her into the master bathroom and switched

on the light. "Clean towel," he said as he opened a linen closet. "I'll leave some clothes for you on the bed."

Her eyes were wide in her pale face. "You're not going to ask me why I'm here?"

His smile was soft, and it took every ounce of his willpower not to reach out and touch her. "Shower first. Talk later. With vodka. *Da?*"

"*Da*," she replied with a smile of her own.

He closed the bathroom door and let out a breath. After laying out a pair of sweatpants and a thermal shirt, he went back into the living room and flipped on the gas fireplace. He poured a glass of vodka and drank it while staring out at the gray sky and sheets of rain that splattered against the window.

"Can I get one of those?" Maryruth asked, startling him. He hadn't heard her approach. Bracing himself, he turned. Her wet hair was combed back from her face. She looked innocent and young. She *was* young, he reminded himself. But not so innocent. He didn't care, he realized. He'd tried to be angry at her, for her relationship with Auggie, but when she'd told him the story of how it had come to be, he found he couldn't fault her.

He poured a glass and held it out to her. She hesitated before taking the few steps to his outstretched hand. When she moved to take a seat by the fire, he shook his head.

"This chair is more comfortable," he said, gesturing to the black leather club chair.

Clutching her glass, she curled up in the chair, pulling her bare toes underneath her. "Thank you," she said quietly. "I—"

"Drink," he commanded.

She drank.

Igor took a seat in the opposite facing chair and watched her. Maryruth looked around the apartment, as if noticing the decor for the first time. "Nice place," she said.

"Thank you."

He could tell she wanted to ask him what he did for a living, to be able to afford such luxury. At the bathhouse one long Saturday ago, he'd told her he was in the family business and had left it at that.

They sat in silence for a few moments before he asked, "How did you find me?"

She traced the rim of her glass with her index finger. "I went to the bathhouse. I figured if you could find out about me, I could do the same. A nice gentleman by the name of Sasha Petrovich gave me your contact information, no questions asked."

"Ah, Sasha. Yes."

"Friend of yours?" she gathered.

"Yes." He took a sip of vodka and didn't elaborate.

She frowned in contemplation before obviously deciding to speak. "You know when you came to Long Island to see me and I told you the reason I didn't show up at the bathhouse that day was because Auggie'd had a crisis?"

"Yes."

"I lied."

"Did you?"

"When you kissed me," she exhaled, "it was like everything I didn't know I could feel exploded inside of me. It terrified the hell out of me."

"That's why you ran? Because you were afraid of feeling?"

She shook her head and lowered her gaze in shame. "I ran because your kiss threatened my entire way of life."

He gripped the glass in his hand, knowing if he clasped

it too much tighter it would shatter. He forced himself to loosen his hold. "Explain."

"I'm a small-town girl…living in a lonely world." She smiled, but her humor faded when Igor didn't return her grin. "I have a high school education—and a famous painter wanted me. *Me.* He exposed me to the world, Igor. Introduced me to food and wine, culture, art. I had nothing to offer him except my looks. I knew one day Auggie would find someone else—another muse."

"Is that what brought you to my door?" Igor asked. "He found another?"

She shook her head. "He let me go."

"What?"

"He said our time together had run its course and that I was free to explore and live my life—without him." She hunched in the chair and stared into the clear liquid. "Have you ever felt lost and found at the same time?"

He didn't know how to answer. He wasn't sure she wanted him to. "Did you come here because you needed a place to stay?"

She looked up at him, her eyes narrowing and then softening. "I don't blame you for thinking that. But no. I didn't come here because I needed a place to stay. Auggie… He…took care of me."

"Then why are you here?" He needed to know. He needed to hear her say it.

"Because I want to be," she said simply.

Igor didn't make a move to get up, nor did she. They finished their vodka in silence, staring into the fire, thinking of the possibilities.

Chapter 10

"You mean to tell me," Sasha said, gripping his too expensive to-go cup of coffee, "that Maryruth spent the night last night and *nothing* happened."

"Something happened," Igor stated. "Just not sex."

"Why the fuck not? You've been chasing this girl for months. I almost hand-deliver her to your door and you didn't do anything?"

"I'm not a predator," Igor growled. "I have some manners."

"I've seen the way you treat women. You have no manners. And very little class."

"Different. I had no desire to marry any of them."

Sasha stopped walking. Surly Brooklynites flipped him the bird and cursed at him. Sasha appeared not to notice, his gaze intense and focused on Igor.

"Wait just a fucking minute," Sasha said. "You can't be serious."

Igor raised an eyebrow but said nothing.

Sasha grasped Igor's arm and moved him out of the line of traffic. "You don't even know her."

"I know her."

"Yeah, you know she was with some other guy this entire time."

Igor knew how it looked. But there were some things he wasn't going to explain. His complex feelings for Maryruth were one of them. "Why did you give her my address?"

"Because I knew you wanted her. I didn't think it was more than that…"

"Just wait," Igor said lightly.

"For what?"

"For when a woman comes along, knocks the wind out of you, gets under your skin. There won't be enough vodka or other women to make your forget her."

Sasha rolled his eyes. "Doubtful. One woman is pretty much the same as the next."

Igor laughed, feeling lighter than he had in years. He didn't know what the future held for him and Maryruth, but he was surprisingly hopeful.

Though he hadn't touched her last night and she'd slept in the guest room, she'd still been there in the morning. They'd stared at each other over their mugs of coffee, not saying much, not needing to.

Sasha and Igor started walking again. The day had dawned gray and overcast, but the sun was coming out, drying the plants and trees. It already promised to be a very green spring.

Sasha brought him back to reality when he asked, "What are you going to do about Katarina?"

"I don't know."

"And Olaf?"

Igor couldn't think about his father. If Igor didn't follow through and marry Katarina, Olaf would lose power, lose standing with the Drugovs and the Dolinsky leadership would be tenuous.

"Let's focus on the matter at hand, shall we?" Igor asked, turning the conversation to the upcoming meeting with the Poles.

Olaf had decided to take Igor's advice and discuss the possibility of getting in on the ground floor of the Greenpoint real estate market. Properties were cheap because Greenpoint wasn't as convenient to Manhattan as Williamsburg, which was right over the bridge. But in a few years' time, when Williamsburg was maxed out, people would be looking to move. By that time, there would hopefully be enough of a transportation infrastructure to support the neighborhood of Greenpoint.

Olaf was sending Sasha and Igor to meet with Aleksy Kowal, the head of the Polish mafia. It wasn't that Olaf trusted Igor to handle it, but more about the fact that he didn't trust the Poles. He did business with outsiders only because he had to in order to grow his empire.

Sasha and Igor arrived at a Polish travel agency. The signs and pictures placed in the windows were dated and faded. Sasha opened the front door and Igor stepped inside first. There were three desks, all with old Macintosh computers, a fax/copy machine, and a wealth of florescent lighting.

"Sure we have the right place?" Sasha asked quietly, looking around.

A young woman wearing a black skirt and white button-down shirt entered the room through a back door. She smiled. "Mr. Dolinsky?"

"*Da.*"

"Right this way," she said.

They followed her to the door that led to a private room, which was equipped with expensive furniture, a coffee and end table, and a big screen TV. This was where the real business was conducted—the travel agency was just a front.

Aleksy Kowal, a man at least fifteen years older than both Sasha and Igor, stood up from one of the brown leather couches, his black suit jacket unbuttoned. Igor reached out to shake his hand.

"Thank you for coming," Aleksy said in heavily accented English.

"Thank you for having us," Igor said, just as polite.

"Can I offer you something to drink? Coffee? Water?"

"Coffee, please," Igor said and then looked at Sasha.

"Same for me."

Aleksy nodded at the young woman and then said something in Polish. She left, the door clicking shut.

"Please." Aleksy gestured to two vacant leather chairs.

Igor and Sasha sat.

"Your trip from Manhattan," he began. "It was pleasant?"

"We took public transportation," Igor stated. "And then we spent the morning walking around. I wanted to get a feel for the neighborhood."

Aleksy smiled. "Did you visit one of Greenpoint's many bakeries?"

"Not yet," Igor admitted. "Though I would love a restaurant recommendation for lunch."

They chatted amiably for a few minutes before the young woman knocked on the door and then entered. She carried a tray with three cups of steaming coffee, cream, sugar, and a plate of baked goods. She set the tray down and then quietly left.

"Try the *makowiec*," Aleksy said, gesturing to the poppy-seed cake. "My mother's recipe."

Sasha picked up a piece of *makowiec* and took a bite. "Delicious."

Aleksy beamed and then turned serious. "Now, let's discuss business."

An hour later, Sasha and Igor left the travel agency. Aleksy Kowal drove a hard bargain, but so did Igor. Both parties walked away happy and satisfied.

Sasha walked away with the young woman's phone number.

"You're unbelievable," Igor said with a laugh, following Aleksy's directions to the restaurant he'd recommended.

"Just trying to build good will between our nations," Sasha quipped.

Igor shook his head. "You're buying lunch."

Chapter 11

Maryruth was right where he left her that morning—curled up on his couch with a mug of tea. She was still in his sweats, his socks on her feet. Setting down the magazine she'd been flipping through, she turned her attention to him.

"How did the business meeting go?" she asked.

"Good," he said, shrugging out of his suit jacket and hanging it on the back of a chair. Igor hadn't expounded on what his business entailed and thankfully, she hadn't asked.

"How are you feeling?"

"Okay. I think." She sighed.

"Talk to me," he offered, taking a seat next to her on the couch.

"It'll sound dumb."

"No. I doubt that."

She bit her lip and brushed her blond hair off her shoulders. It was a tangled mess, and he was glad she wasn't the type of woman who had to appear perfect all the time. He knew what she looked like going to bed, knew how she looked in the morning.

"I think I want to go to college."

He blinked. "That's not dumb."

"Really?"

"Really."

"But it feels so...average. Normal. And my life has been anything but."

"Which is why it might be good for you. I think it's a brilliant idea."

She smiled and looked relieved.

"How long," he asked quietly.

"What?"

"How long were you living Auggie's dream and not your own?"

"Ah." She brought the mug of tea to her lips but at the last moment decided not to take a sip. "It was amazing for those first few months. New. Exciting. This older man…" She looked at him. "Are you sure you want to hear this?"

He nodded. He wanted to know everything. Ignorance was never bliss. Whoever had thought up that statement was a fucking moron.

"It was about him. Always. His wants, his needs, his muse, his demands. It was exhausting. I gave it all to him, you know? So what was left for me? Nothing."

"You came to my door last night and you were crying," he reminded her. "You looked devastated and heartbroken.

"It was relief," she admitted quietly. "I was crying in relief."

"Oh," he said because he didn't know what else to say.

"I didn't know it was relief, though. Not until I had a good night's sleep and realized I didn't have to get up and be anything to anyone. I was finally able to just be *me* and think about what I wanted, when I wanted it."

"And what you want now is to go to college, yes?"

She nodded. "I just…want to learn, you know? Absorb all this knowledge and figure out what I'm good at, what I love. Because I don't know any of those things. I didn't have a family that encouraged growth. It's part of why I left, I think. I figured out a lot of things away from them and then as I got wrapped up in Auggie, I didn't have to figure out anything. I'd had a momentary purpose."

"I know what that's like," he admitted slowly.

"I'm tired of hiding. Tired of not knowing who I am or what I want. I'm ready to figure it out."

"You're pretty resilient. You know that, don't you?"

"Kind of have to be." She smiled, but it wasn't in humor. "You can't rely on anyone else to save you. Misplaced faith."

Sometimes, you can't even rely on yourself, he didn't say. Instead he said, "Have you eaten yet today?"

∽

"Tell me something," Maryruth said after she pushed away an empty plate.

"Tell you what?" Igor took the dish and placed it in the dishwasher. He could've left it in the sink and the housekeeper would've taken care of it, but he was an adult and not a slob.

"Where the hell did you learn how to cook like that?"

He looked over his shoulder at her and smiled. "Liked it, eh?"

"Loved it. You could be a chef."

His smile slipped.

She frowned. "What did I say?"

"Nothing. It's not you."

"Then what?"

"According to my mother, I could've been a great many things," he admitted.

"Never too late."

He threw her a wry smile. "So you've told me before."

"What else are you good at?"

Igor raised a suggestive eyebrow, causing them both to laugh. There was an easy intimacy between them; when she ebbed, he flowed. When she waxed, he waned. He knew they were right together, knew it in his bones. But he wasn't going to push her for anything more at the moment. She wasn't ready; she was still reeling from her separation.

Whoever had come before him didn't matter; Igor Dolinsky was going to be her last. And he could wait.

"Hello? Igor?" Maryruth asked. "Did you hear my question?"

His eyes came back into focus. "Sorry. Yes. You asked what else I'm good at?"

She nodded.

He paused a moment and then, "Follow me." She trailed after him into the living room. He gestured for her to take a seat on the couch. When she was curled up and comfortable, he retrieved the old, battered viola case from the hall closet. He hated that he kept it tucked away and out of sight. One moment in time, the viola had been an extension of himself, as necessary as a limb.

"Oh," she breathed when he revealed the instrument to her.

He told her the story of how the viola had come to the family. She listened with rapt attention. Finally, he was silent as he put the viola to his shoulder and tuned his beloved instrument. Igor spent a moment saying hello after a long absence.

As Igor played a mournful ballad, he felt the ice around his heart begin to thaw. This time, he let it. It was truly exhausting holding himself back from living, from loving.

When he played the final note, the sudden silence felt deafening. He slowly opened his eyes, afraid of what he'd see.

Maryruth was frozen like a marble statue. If not for the tears streaming down her cheeks, Igor would've thought his music had done nothing for her.

"Put down the viola," she said through a strained throat.

He did so without question. The moment his hands were free, Maryruth leapt up from her seat and launched herself at him. Igor grunted when he hit the floor, but he didn't care because Maryruth was on top of him, her hands cradling his cheeks.

"I'm in so much trouble," she murmured.

Igor let out a strangled chuckle. "You? I've been in trouble since the moment we met."

Her smile was brighter than a solar flare. Throwing her head back, she shouted with laughter. She leaned over and rubbed her nose against Igor's. Her eyelashes fluttered against his skin and he closed his eyes, savoring the feel of her in his arms.

"Tell me about that piece."

He opened his eyes. "What about it?"

"It meant something to you." She brushed the drying tears from her cheeks and sat back but didn't move to get off him.

"It was the song I composed for my mother's funeral."

She let out a long sigh.

"My father wouldn't let me play it."

Her face contorted into fury. "I hate your father. How could he?"

He shrugged.

"That's not an answer!" she snapped, her hands fisting in righteous anger. "You were a child who had just lost his mother, and you composed, *composed*, a tribute to her and he wouldn't let you share it?"

He took one of her fisted hands and brought it to his mouth and placed a kiss on her knuckles. "Thank you, *pchelka*."

Her face softened. "What does that mean?"

"It means 'bee'. It's a Russian endearment."

"Oh."

"Now, *pchelka*, I'm going to ask you to either kiss me or get off me. And if you do get off me, will you grab me an icepack? I think I bruised something."

Chapter 12

They spent the rest of the evening entwined on the couch, holding hands, talking. There was no discussion of Maryruth leaving his apartment. Where would she stay, a hotel? Igor wouldn't hear of it—not that she was putting up much of a fight.

"But I do need clothes of my own," she said. "I can't keep wearing yours."

"Why not?" He brushed a lock of hair away from her face. "You look beautiful in my clothes."

She smiled in pleasure, but then the grin faded from her lips. "Igor," she began.

"Maryruth."

"I won't jump from one man to another," she stated. "I won't do that to myself. Or to you."

"All right," he said easily.

She frowned. "I don't understand you at all."

"Good. That keeps it interesting."

Maryruth chuckled. "Seriously. What am I going to do with you?"

"When you're ready, I have a few ideas."

"What if it takes me months to be ready?" she asked, sidestepping his innuendo.

"Then I'll wait. However long it takes." Leaning towards her, he pressed his forehead to hers and stared into her eyes. "You're worth the wait, Maryruth."

"How can you say that?" she whispered, her breath teasing the skin of his cheeks. "Look what kind of baggage I dropped at your front door."

He didn't even want to get into the type of baggage he had.

Igor didn't want to frighten her with the intensity of his feelings, not so soon after her last experience. She needed to feel through her emotions before she would truly be open again.

"I'll wait," he repeated because that was all he could say.

"Why?"

"Because."

She flung her arms around him and pressed her face to his shoulder.

Perhaps waiting months for Maryruth wouldn't be the worst thing in the world. It would give him time to tell his father that he wouldn't be marrying Katarina Drugov. It would give him time to protect his balls from Katarina. Though she'd agreed to a sham engagement, he knew if he told her he wanted to go through with the marriage, she would be happy.

"Why did you sigh?" Maryruth asked, pulling back.

"Just thinking about things. Other things," he clarified.

"Cryptic."

"*Da.*"

She climbed off the couch and padded her way towards the kitchen. "Do you have any chocolate?"

"No."

"Ice cream?"
"No."
"Cookies?"
"No."

She looked over her shoulder at him. "Why not? What's wrong with you?"

"Me? It's dinner time. What's wrong with *you*?"

Maryruth laughed. "Fair enough. But seriously, do you have anything sweet in here?"

"Honey. From Upstate."

She rolled her eyes. "That's not what I meant."

"I could have Charlie send out for something."

"Charlie?"

"The doorman."

"Ah, no. That's okay."

"What happened to all your clothes?" he asked, changing the subject.

"They're still at Auggie's. I'll go back and get them. When I'm ready."

"I have an idea," he said.

"I'm listening."

"Why don't you take a bath? I'll have Charlie run out and get you ice cream. What's your flavor of choice?"

"Vanilla bean."

"Really? That's so…"

"Boring?"

"Traditional," he corrected. "I assumed you'd want something more exotic."

She smiled but said nothing.

"Bath?" he urged. "I have a Jacuzzi tub in the master bathroom."

"Trying to spoil me?" she teased.

"Something like that."

They gazed at one another until finally Maryruth pulled her eyes away. "Thank you," she said quietly.

"You're welcome."

With one final look, she left the room. Igor picked up the phone to call Charlie and asked him to bring him different brands of vanilla bean ice cream. He wanted to give Maryruth choices.

After hanging up, he took a seat on the couch. Worry gnawed at him. For the moment, he and Maryruth were safely cocooned in a bubble of isolation. They only person who knew about them was Sasha, and he would never betray him.

Before Igor told Olaf that he wouldn't marry Katarina, he needed to speak with the woman first. Maybe it would all work out and everyone would get everything they wanted—without a marriage alliance.

He snorted at his delusional hope. Igor wasn't stupid. He was about to seriously rock the boat. Glancing in the direction of his bedroom, he knew it was all going to be worth it.

A knock sounded on the door. He got up and answered it. "That was fast," he said, the smile on his face dying when he saw that it wasn't Charlie with the ice cream.

"I'll show you fast," Katarina rasped seductively, draping her arms around his neck and brushing her lips against his.

He took a step back, trying to disengage her hold on him. "What are you doing here?" he asked in dreaded confusion.

She frowned. "I told the doorman that your fiancée wanted to surprise you. So, surprise!"

"Fiancée?" came the soft question from somewhere behind him.

Igor turned. Maryruth stood in the living room,

wearing his robe, her hair pulled up into a bun, her expression crestfallen.

"*Da*," Katarina said, her gaze narrowing as she looked down her nose at Maryruth. "His fiancée. And you are?"

"I don't know," she mumbled, turning away, shoulders hunched.

Igor shut the front door. "Katarina, will you give us a moment?"

She shrugged her shoulders.

"Pour yourself a drink," he commanded before stalking after Maryruth who had disappeared into his bedroom.

He found her sitting on the edge of the half-full tub. The water had been shut off, and there was only the *drip, drip* of the last drops of water splashing into the bath.

"You have a fiancée." She looked at him with accusatory eyes—all traces of defeat were gone.

"No, well, not really." He sighed. It was going to be difficult to explain. Would she believe him?

"Not really?" Maryruth parroted. "I'm not an idiot, Igor. I may have been acting like one, but I'm not stupid. That woman has some sort of claim on you."

"Our parents want us to get married," he shot out rapidly. "Katarina and I agreed to a fake engagement but have no intention of going through with it."

Maryruth rolled her eyes and stood. "I think I should leave. You need to be alone with your *fiancée*."

"She's not my fiancée!" he yelled, finally losing his patience.

"Then maybe you should be the one to set her straight!" Maryruth yelled back. "Because she thinks she is. I saw the way she looked at you!"

"I don't care how Kat looks at me. I care how *you* look at me!"

"This is so fucking twisted," Maryruth panted. "This won't work. I need to be on my own for a while."

"Oh great," Igor sneered, his face contorting into an ugly snarl. "What a fucking excuse. You're a goddamn coward."

"You don't know anything about me. You're just like Auggie. You've put me on this pedestal—I'm not some trinket, an adornment to appease your ego, Igor."

"You're the one who doesn't know *me*," he said, his voice steely. His eyes flashed with anger, but he pulled it back, pulled it in. To fully unleash it would be catastrophic.

"Have you slept with her?"

"Why does that matter?"

She fell silent.

He sighed. "Yes. Kat and I have been together. So what? You were with Auggie when we met, when I kissed you outside the bathhouse."

She stared at him, faced him head on when she admitted, "I won't survive you, Igor."

He took a step closer. "You won't have to."

She closed the rest of the distance between them. "Promise?"

"Promise. I just need some time—my father expects things. Kat's parents expect things. This is delicate."

She nodded. "All right."

"I don't have a fiancée."

"I believe you."

He raised an eyebrow.

She stood on her toes and kissed him. Open mouth, tongue, and feeling.

His arms wrapped around her, hauled her closer. "You're far from perfect," he growled against her lips.

Maryruth smiled against his skin. "You mean that?"

He deepened the kiss and silenced her.

They were tempered volatility. She consumed him, body and heart. He'd give her everything he had if only she'd let him.

Moments later, they returned to the present and separated. They held onto each other, sucking in air like they were dying.

"Take a bath," he urged, reluctantly releasing her. "Don't think of anything except what just happened between us."

She bit her lip and stepped back. "What about Katarina?"

"I'll deal with Katarina."

Chapter 13

Katarina stood at the kitchen counter, a glass of vodka in her slender hand. Her sleek black hair shone under the light, her cheekbones high, perfect shadows on the apples of her cheeks. She was gorgeous—could've been a model. And yet, such perfection held no allure for him.

"So that's the woman," she said without a trace of bitterness.

"Excuse me?"

She cocked her head to the side. "Remember the night of the opera? And you asked about love and marriage."

"You laughed at me."

"Well, the joke is on me, isn't it?" She took a dainty sip of her drink.

"You're not mad?" he pressed.

"How could I be mad? We both agreed we're not really engaged. It bought us a few months of freedom, but now we have to tell our parents."

"I'd been hoping to avoid this moment a while longer," he admitted.

She smiled, showing straight, white teeth.

"I want to speak to your father—directly," Igor said.

"Before or after you speak to *your* father?"

He paused in thought. "Before." If he could find a way to make good on the alliance without marrying Kat, then Olaf would not have any cause for worry. Igor had no desire to anger the temperamental Russian beast that was his father. It would probably occur no matter what. When Olaf didn't get his way, he acted like a petulant child.

"I don't envy you," she said. "I was prepared to go through with the marriage."

"If business needs a marriage to secure a partnership then it must not be strong enough on its own."

"You know how things are done in our families," she reminded him. "Does she know?"

Igor shook his head. "No. Not yet."

"You have to tell her. She can't go into this with her eyes closed."

"I know." He sighed. "I just need some time."

His cell phone rang, and he pulled it out his pocket. He grimaced. Olaf's name flashed across the screen. "Guess that's out of the question, *da*?"

She smiled without humor and threw back the rest of her vodka before saying, "*Da.*"

He silenced his phone.

"I'm impressed," Kat said. "That was a bold move."

"Or stupid." He never ignored Olaf's calls. To ignore them would incite rage and instability. "Would your father be willing to meet with me?"

"I wouldn't see why not."

Igor wanted to face Viktor Drugov as a man—it was his duty to explain even though Igor wouldn't be marrying Kat, there was no reason to fold the alliance.

"Is she worth it?" Kat asked quietly, eyes steady.

He nodded.

"I'll speak to my father first. And then you'll speak to him. I'm sure we can all come to a reasonable understanding."

He heard her tone. He would pay for breaking the engagement. But he would give anything for his freedom.

~

It was the day of reckoning; the day Igor was going to tell Olaf he wouldn't be marrying Kat. Father and son trekked to their customary restaurant where they had lunch every Sunday after church. Olaf was in a pleasant mood, and Igor hoped he'd be in an even better mood after they ate.

Igor waited until the end of the meal, and he didn't mince words. "Kat and I will not be getting married."

Olaf's fork was halfway to his mouth with a bite of *ptichie moloko*, a traditional Russian dessert. His brown eyes narrowed with anger as his fist clenched metal.

Igor blazed on. "I've already spoken to Kat's father. Though he was disappointed, he still wants to go through with the merger."

The fork hit the plate, and Olaf shoved back from the table. He stood, looming over his son. "You disrespectful *derrmo*. You went behind my back!"

"No," Igor said, still calm, still rational. "I handled the matter to my satisfaction."

His father's face fused red before he punched Igor in the eye. The force knocked Igor back, his chair tilting onto two legs. In an attempt to right himself, he grasped the tablecloth, but it wouldn't hold him. Igor went down and brought dishes, glassware, and *ptichie moloko* with him.

"Restitution," Olaf seethed, standing over his son.

Igor didn't bother trying to stand, choosing to stay down. No reason to give his father another reason to deck him.

"Hear me?"

Igor nodded.

Olaf grumbled, turned, and walked out of the restaurant. With a sigh, Igor finally rose. The few occupants of the restaurant stared at their plates and pretended like they hadn't seen anything.

The elderly owner of the restaurant came to him, took Igor's arm with a gnarled hand, and gently led him to the back kitchen.

"Thank you, Boris," Igor said in Russian to the man who helped him clean up.

"I look forward to the day when you are leader," Boris said, staring at Igor with shrewd blue eyes.

Igor patted Boris's hand, his mind shifting from cleaning *ptichie moloko* from his shirt to more pressing matters. His thoughts began to churn.

～

"You don't have to do this," Sasha said. "Just challenge him. Now. End this. You have enough supporters to back your claim."

Igor shoved a change of gym clothes into a bag. "It's not the right time."

Sasha growled in frustration at his best friend. "Not the right time? You're about to enter The Arena. There will be bets on how many teeth you lose, how long it takes for you to go down, and if you'll be pissing blood by the end of the night. Don't. Do. This."

Igor stopped and looked at Sasha. "Have to. If I don't, Olaf will know about the dissension. The last thing I want is a bloody take over."

"It will be bloody no matter what. Your father will not step down. He'd sooner kill you than see you succeed—not until he's ready for you."

The door to Igor's bedroom was closed, and locked, just in case Maryruth came home and decided to come looking for him. He hoped he was able to leave before seeing her. The last thing he wanted to do was lie to her— but she couldn't know about where he was going, or what was about to happen. Though she'd know soon enough— he wouldn't be able to hide his injuries from her. Telling her he was going on a business trip while recovering in a hotel room sounded like the smart thing to do. Igor sat down on his bed.

"There has to be another way," Sasha stated again.

"You want to fight in my stead? Or better yet, offer to marry Kat?"

"I don't think Kat's father wants a second-in-command for his daughter." Sasha snorted. "Besides, you've had her already. My future wife will not be your cast-off."

"Very well, then." He stood and grabbed his gym bag.

"How do you know this isn't a setup?"

"I don't. Not for sure. But I'm counting on one thing."

"What's that?"

"My father has spent years hating me while simultaneously grooming me to be his successor. To kill me now would cause too many problems."

"Anarchy. We'd all revolt."

"Promise me something," Igor said.

"What?" Sasha asked warily.

"Not a word of this to Maryruth."

The two friends stared each other down.

"I'll tell her," Igor stated. "When I think she's ready."

Sasha ran a hand across his jaw. "Dangerous games we're playing."

Resolve flashed across Igor's face. "*Da.* But I intend to win."

Chapter 14

The Arena was an underground fighting ring. Men of the streets, men of crime, took to The Arena to settle disputes in the time-honored tradition of a theatrical battle.

Two men would go into the ring, armed with nothing but their bodies and minds, and fight until one was no longer standing. Some died. Some didn't. Those that lived knew what they were made of.

It smelled of sweat, testosterone, and blood. Igor wasn't the only one fighting that evening. A decent-sized crowd had already gathered to watch two men currently engaged in a duel. Most of the patrons were men, but there were a few women present, clinging to their protectors and looking around like they wanted to be anywhere than where they were.

Bookies were taking bets, yelling over the sounds of flesh smacking on flesh.

The large, brass bell rang in rapid succession as the referee called out the winner of the most recent match. A stocky, robust fellow with cauliflower ears raised a bloody hand. The throng went wild.

This was The Arena and the men who fought were gladiators.

Igor came out of the dressing room, garbed in a white t-shirt and a pair of black gym shorts. Sasha was standing by the water fountain waiting for him. Igor moved forward, his friend trailing ever so slightly behind him.

"He's in the glass box, yeah?" Igor asked without taking his eyes off of Sasha. He would not give Olaf the satisfaction of showing him anything less than a composed successor.

"*Da*. Kat and her parents are with him."

"Of course." He flexed his fists. "Do you know who I'm fighting?"

"Vlad Yevtukh. A Ukrainian. He's…"

"What?"

"Huge," Sasha finished grimly. He gestured to the gargantuan man waiting his turn outside the corner of the ring.

Igor had already popped four aspirin and four Ibuprofen in preparation. If it hadn't been illegal, Igor would've procured a drug on the black market that would dull his pain while he fought. Then again, pain was the body's way of expressing itself—and drugs in The Arena were forbidden. No advantages, for anyone. Not even for the son of the Russian mob leader.

Igor sighed. "Let's do this."

Sasha stalked over to the referee and whispered something in the man's ear. He nodded, his face showing his excitement. After announcing Igor and Vlad, he asked them to come forward.

Vlad slipped into the ring, removed his black silk robe, and tossed it at a small crony behind him. His dark eyes watched Igor approach, his face devoid of emotion.

Igor choked down the fear that threatened to consume

him, refusing to show it to the audience, his father, or his opponent. He'd had his nose broken once or twice, back when he was a small, sensitive kid who had been a target for bullies. He'd grown up, toughened up, learned self-defense—had become an alpha.

He slipped into a role and tuned out the cheering audience. He couldn't see them anyway, not with the garish overhead lights.

Igor focused on Vlad. He wouldn't know the man's weaknesses until they started to spar.

The bell rang.

The two men lunged for each other in a brutal display of violence. Igor fought with every instinct he possessed; he pounded, he crunched bone, he spilled blood.

Vlad gave it back to him.

Sweat poured into Igor's swelling eyes. He struggled to take in air through his broken nose. He was tiring, fast. His speed and flexibility were no match for Vlad's brute strength.

How did Jack fell the giant?

He chopped down the beanstalk.

With the last of his energy, Igor crouched and drove his body into Vlad's knees. The man had been expecting an attack of a different nature and hadn't seen Igor's ploy until it was too late. Losing his balance, he gripped Igor's hair and yanked. But Igor would not be defeated. Gritting his teeth, he rammed Vlad into the side of the ring. The behemoth bounced off the springs, ricocheted back towards Igor, his hands outstretched and ready. At the last moment, Igor moved to the side, stuck out his foot and tripped Vlad. The giant went down into a sprawling heap, but before he could get up, Igor sent a swift kick to both of Vlad's kidneys.

The fight ended with a ring of the bell. Triumphant,

Igor maneuvered his adrenaline-pumped body out of the ring and stalked to the dressing room. He locked himself in a bathroom stall before he puked up three Red Bulls and a healthy dose of fear.

~

He had never wanted a woman more than he wanted one right then. He didn't care what she looked like, how old she was, or if she found him attractive.

His body throbbed with pain and bloodlust. He leaned against the cool wall of the dressing room and closed his eyes. He needed a woman before the pain settled into him and rendered him useless.

"Igor?"

He lifted his bloody, bruised limbs from the wall and turned.

Maryruth stood a few feet from him. Her blond hair was pulled back into a ponytail. The bright lights overhead made her look pale. Or maybe she was pale because all the blood had drained from her face.

"What are you doing here?" he rasped. His gaze left her eyes to drag down her body. She wore a pair of dark jeans, flats, a light peacoat. Completely out of place in a sinner's den.

He wanted to drag his tongue along the column of her throat, taste her skin, mar it with his blood. The primitive picture took hold of him until he was reaching for her. He forced his hands down.

"Get out," he gritted.

"You're hurt."

"*Da.*"

"Let me help you." Her eyes widened as she pleaded.

"I'll hurt you, if you stay."

She took a step closer. "You need me."

He didn't correct her.

"You need me the way a man needs a woman." Her eyes dropped to the bulge in his shorts. "So take me."

"You don't know what you're offering." One last chance. He'd give her one last chance before he pounced, took her body, used her to satisfy himself.

"I know," she said quietly. "You won't break me."

If he touched her, he'd make sure they both went up in flames. He'd torch everything inside of her, reducing her to a pile of ashes and lust. If he touched her, she might survive, only to leave him. Still, better to know now...

"Take me, Igor. I'm yours."

He lunged for her, grasping her arms and hauling her to him. His lips crushed hers, forcing them open, invading her mouth with his tongue. He felt like a conqueror, beating the weak into submission.

Before he knew it, she was shoving him against the wall, claiming his mouth as her own.

He growled.

A conqueror needed a queen by his side.

His fingers ripped the hair tie from her ponytail, spilling blond tresses down her back. He gripped her thick hair and tugged, forcing her mouth from his. His teeth nipped at her neck, his tongue bathing the throbbing pulse of her blood.

He released her and went for her jeans, needing them off, needing to feel the hot silk of her skin, needing to feel her wetness.

The vixen wore a black lace thong.

He shredded it in one move. Maryruth shuddered.

"Wall," he commanded. "Hands on the wall."

She nearly tripped in her eagerness to do as he commanded. She pressed her cheek and hands to the wall, giving him her backside, giving him her trust, giving him her body.

He'd pay homage to her later. Now to rut.

His hands shoved down his gym shorts and boxers in one swift move. Taking himself in hand, he stroked his hard, hot length a few times. He was more than primed, more than ready.

Was she?

He reached around, his fingers finding the entrance to her body. She was hot and ready, moaning her want for him. She leaned over, presenting herself like a sacrifice.

Igor slammed into her. He'd never felt anything like this. Hot, wet, tight, *his*.

She squirmed against him, groaning out her pleasure.

His hands slipped up her sweater to tease her already hardened nipples.

"More," she gasped as he continued his relentless pillage. "I need more."

He gave it to her, hard and fast, slick and hot. Igor was past words, past anything but feeling her body holding onto his in a relentless grip.

"Harder!" she yelled.

One hand clutched her waist as the other moved to the front of her. He rubbed in circles until she was punching the wall with her closed fists, coming fiercely and loudly around him. With a few more mindless, aching thrusts, he slammed into her a final time and came with a guttural shout.

Igor collapsed against her, pressed his head to her shoulder blade and tried to keep his heart from jumping out of his ribs.

She shivered, her body clasping him.

He shuddered and slowly eased out of her. Igor bent to pull up his boxers and shorts, already feeling his body start to betray him. In another hour, he wouldn't be able to move.

Maryruth turned to face him. Her cheeks were pink, her lips were plump, and her eyes gleamed under the bright lights. She didn't bother trying to restore order to her hair.

Reality came rushing back and shame flooded Igor.

She reached out to grasp his chin in her delicate, slim fingers, forcing him to look at her. She gently pressed her lips to his before pulling back.

"Let's get you home."

Chapter 15

With Sasha's help, they slipped out the back, avoiding the fray and more importantly, Olaf. Though there were tons of unanswered questions—from both sides—Igor and Maryruth waited to speak. Igor's head pounded, his body ached, and he could barely see or breathe.

He needed a doctor.

Sasha and Maryruth got him home and into the shower. Igor leaned and slumped against the wall. Sasha and Maryruth exchanged a look.

"Ah, I think you might be better equipped to help him," Sasha remarked dryly.

"Maybe you call the doctor, while I help him?" she suggested.

"A good plan."

Sasha gave them privacy. Maryruth stripped off Igor's soiled, bloody clothes and cast them aside before undressing herself. She turned on the faucet, splashing lukewarm water over them.

"As hot as you can stand," Igor rasped. He didn't know

if his eyes were closed or just swollen shut. After the shower, Sasha and Maryruth got Igor into bed.

The doctor arrived and did an examination, told him to watch for blood in his urine, but otherwise to rest, take a lot of painkillers, and call it a day.

"Olaf has been calling your phone non-stop," Sasha said. "How do you want me to handle it?"

"Don't do anything," Igor said. Something cool hit his eyes, and he felt instant relief. He managed to get some pills down his throat and then leaned back against the pillow.

"Take care of him," he heard Sasha say to Maryruth.

"I will. Sasha…thanks."

His friend's retreating steps echoed in his ears, followed by the bedroom door closing.

"Let's talk," Igor said. There were things he needed to know. How she'd gotten into The Arena, how she'd tracked him, if she was leaving now that she knew he wasn't what he seemed.

"Tomorrow," she promised.

He paused. "You'll still be here?"

"Yes."

He fell into a deep sleep, awoke sometime in the night, and stumbled his way to the bathroom. He was shaking and violently ill by the time he made it, but he did it on his own two legs.

No blood in his urine, thank God.

He nearly crawled his way back to bed, falling onto his side and shuddering.

"Igor?" Maryruth's voice was rough with sleep.

He was doomed to a life of pain. That voice, whispered in the middle of the night, had him hard and ready.

"I'm fine," he gritted, his hand going to his side.

The lamp turned on and suddenly she was there, next

to him. She'd been sleeping in his bed, and he hadn't even been aware of it.

"Where does it hurt?"

"Everywhere."

"Right, sorry."

Through cracked eyelids, he watched her get out of bed. A moment later, she returned with a glass of water and a handful of pills. He managed to swallow them before leaning back, exhausted.

She crawled in next to him and gently ran her fingers through his hair.

"Is this okay?" she whispered.

He moaned in pleasure and relief.

"I saw the fight," she said.

"We're doing this? Now?"

"You've got other things you have to do?" she teased. "Like run a marathon?"

He held in a chuckle. "Don't make me laugh."

"Sorry."

Igor inhaled a shallow breath. "So you saw the fight?"

"Yeah. You were…"

Brutal, violent, ruthless?

"Incredible."

He searched for her free hand, found it, and brought it to his lips.

"You aren't who you claim to be either," she pointed out. "What kind of family business are you in, Igor?"

"Do I really have to say it?"

"No, I guess you don't."

He paused before asking, "How did you find me?"

"Followed you."

"Ah, sure. How'd you get in? Security can't be bribed."

"Really? That's unusual."

"Part of The Arena's appeal."

"The Arena?"

He explained the name, he explained its purpose, but he didn't want to get distracted. "So, how did you get in?"

"I told them I was your girlfriend."

"And they bought it?"

"No. Not until I told them they'd be choking on their teeth if you found out that I'd been turned away."

"What did I say about making me laugh?"

"Sorry," she said, a smile in her tone. "They finally let me in, and I…didn't know what to expect. I didn't know what I was walking into. Thank God Sasha spotted me."

"Thank God, indeed."

"He told me not to go into the dressing room. Told me to give you some time to calm down."

"Why didn't you listen?"

"Because you needed me."

"You were selfless in that dressing room."

"Don't think it completely altruistic," she negated. "I was just as ready for what happened between us as you were."

"No regrets?"

"None. A woman wants to be wanted. I'm not a rose petals and candlelight kind of woman, Igor."

"I'm sure I could change your mind on that."

"I'm sure you could." She sobered. "Why were you there to fight?"

"I don't know what I can tell you."

"All of it."

"It might scare you."

"No."

He sighed. "My father wanted a blood payment for breaking my engagement to Kat."

"Why? You weren't really engaged."

"Olaf wanted to show everyone who's in charge of the family business."

"Ah, so you were toeing the line."

He said nothing because to say anything would mean he'd have to explain the politics and the coup in the works. And though he had misgivings about bringing her into his world, he didn't think for a second he could let her walk away. He didn't have it in him to be that selfless.

"Do you …" she started.

"Yes?" he pressed.

"Do you plan on introducing me to your father?"

"Someday. It's inevitable. No doubt he saw you with Sasha—saw you enter the dressing room where I was."

"Should I be afraid of him?" she whispered.

"No, *pchelka*. I'm here. I'll protect you."

Chapter 16

"I'm proud of you, son," Olaf said.

Igor raised an eyebrow but otherwise didn't move from his spot on the sauna bench. Mostly because he was still a colorful array of bruises. His eyes were black, but no longer puffy. His nose was on the mend.

"You handled yourself like a true Dolinsky and took out that Ukrainian giant like it was nothing," Olaf spouted on. "The Drugovs are impressed and still willing to do business with us. Life is good."

Igor remained silent, letting his father's rhetoric blow past him. He wished he didn't feel a small ounce of satisfaction for winning his father's approval. It was something that had always been lacking during Igor's childhood.

"Who's the woman?" Olaf asked with an unusual measure of calm interest.

It didn't fool Igor for a second. "Who would you like her to be?"

"Someone of no importance."

"Sorry to disappoint you."

Father and son stared at one another until Olaf finally

smiled. "She's the reason you risked my wrath. Why you entered The Arena."

"I would shrug, but it would hurt my ribs," Igor quipped.

"You will bring her to my birthday party next week."

Igor pretended to think about it. "*Da.*"

Olaf smiled and slapped his knees before rising. "And on that note, I have a meeting I need to get to." On his way out of the sauna, Olaf stopped in front of Igor. In a rare show of affection, Olaf placed his hand on Igor's shoulder. He didn't say anything, just let his hand linger there before leaving.

Something was brewing. Igor didn't trust Olaf for a moment, and the unusual show of pride and demonstrative display didn't fool him. He needed eyes on his father. The only person he trusted to do that was Sasha.

Igor thought about getting up, but his body refused to move, so instead, he stayed where he was and closed his eyes.

"I could kill you, you know," came an accented voice.

Igor's eyes flew open. He hadn't even heard the sound of the door. Vlad Yevtukh stood over him, his own body a smattering of bruises. His lip was split, and his forehead had a tiny row of stitches, making him look like a Ukrainian Frankenstein.

"So do it and be done with it. At least then I can get back to taking a nap," Igor remarked dryly.

Vlad's dark eyes twinkled, but the man didn't smile. "No. I won't kill you. Not today."

"Glad to hear it. I'm actually pretty fond of living."

At that, Vlad did crack a smile—wincing when he realized it pulled his lips taut. "May I sit?"

"Please." Igor gestured to the bench across from him.

Vlad took a seat and stretched out his long, muscular

legs. "I was undefeated in The Arena. Before we sparred. It made me reevaluate some things…" Vlad clenched and unclenched his left hand. The knuckles were scratched and swollen, but intact.

"I want to be your right-hand man."

"I already have a right-hand man."

"Your left, then. I don't give my allegiance. It has to be won. It would be an honor to serve you. In any way I can."

"Why?" Igor asked. "Don't you have your own interests? Your own people?"

"My people are bloodthirsty and cutthroat. They're too busy backstabbing one another to do anything else. I want to belong. To an empire. One of my choosing."

"And you've chosen mine."

"Not yours. Yet," Vlad pointed out.

"You speak Russian?"

Vlad nodded.

"I don't trust you," Igor stated.

"I know. I can prove myself."

"How?"

"Do you need something handled? Discreetly?" Vlad's dark gaze appeared to see what Igor wouldn't say.

He stood. "Find me when you know you can trust me."

~

Igor opened the door to the apartment and was greeted by unfamiliar sounds and smells.

"Hello?" he called out, dropping his gym bag to the ground and wincing. He really should've considered taping his ribs.

"In the kitchen!" Maryruth yelled back.

He found her at the stove, singing off-key to a Tom Petty song, looking adorable in her leggings and one of his black cashmere sweaters. Three days ago, she'd gone to Long Island to pack up her clothes and other personal belongings. He liked that she chose to wear his clothes even though she had access to her own.

"This is new," Igor said, strolling towards her and placing his hand on her hip. He brushed his lips across hers before leaning over to sniff the contents of a large pot.

"What's new? Someone other than your housekeeper cooking in your kitchen?"

"I cook, if you remember." He playfully swatted her behind. "What are you making?"

"Chicken soup."

"Why?"

She looked at him and rolled her eyes. "Because it's what you feed people when they're sick."

"I'm not sick. I'm injured. Different."

"Whatever, chicken soup is good no matter what. Besides, I add something special to my soup."

"What?"

"Dumplings. Sit. It's almost ready." She waved him over to the table while she ladled out a bowlful of soup. She set it down in front of him. "Might need some salt."

"I'll taste it first," he murmured, his eyes following her movements around the kitchen.

With her hand on the door to the refrigerator, she stopped. "What? Is the soup okay?"

He breathed in the aromatic steam of her chicken soup but didn't reach for his spoon. "I haven't tasted it yet."

"You're looking at me funny."

Igor picked up his utensil, rubbing his thumb along the handle. "I used to revel in the silence of an empty apartment. And now…"

"And now?"

He pointedly looked at her. "Now this apartment feels like a home."

She froze like a woodland creature about to be ensnared by a hunter. Finally, she moved. "When I lived with Auggie," she said softly. "We didn't spend that much time together—outside of when he was painting me. You saw the house." She looked at him for confirmation. He nodded. "We had separate wings. And I spent a lot of time cooking for a man who was too caught up in his art to leave his studio and eat a meal with me."

She sighed. "I like—that we eat together."

He smiled crookedly. He liked more than that.

Chapter 17

That night, Igor and Sasha met on the roof of Igor's apartment complex. It was clear, the air only slightly chilled. They cracked open a bottle of vodka and passed it between them, not bothering with glasses. It was like they were sixteen again, stealing good liquor from their fathers.

Things were different now. For one, only Igor's father was still alive.

"What do you want to talk about first?" Sasha asked, his gaze leaving the lit-up Manhattan skyline to settle on Igor who was seated in a comfortable cushioned patio chair.

"Vlad Yevtukh."

"What he said about the Ukrainians is true. They can't stop fighting long enough to band together to eke out even a small piece of territory."

"They need a true leader."

"Vlad?"

Igor shook his head. "No. Vlad doesn't want to lead. He said as much in our…meeting."

"Do you trust him?" Sasha asked.

"Do you?"

"Not sure yet."

"A test, *da*?" Igor pressed.

"*Da*. What kind of test do you have in mind?"

Igor scratched his jaw in thought. "We want Olaf out of the way, yes?"

"Yes."

"And we want to see if Vlad can be trusted."

"Yes."

Igor paused.

"You're not thinking of having him—"

"No," Igor assured him. "Who's the head of the Ukrainian mafia?"

Sasha threw out a name. "Oh. Oh, I see."

"Death is the cost of entry, no?"

Sasha sighed; the sound was so very Russian.

"What's next on tonight's agenda?" Sasha asked after taking a swig of expensive vodka.

"Olaf's birthday party."

"I heard it will be quite the bash," Sasha drawled.

"He's insisting I bring Maryruth."

"He saw you both together the night of the fight."

"I figured."

"This would've happened sooner or later, right? Unless he was already—"

"Right." Igor took a drink. "She knows, Sasha."

"About us? Our life?"

"Yes. Well, no specifics, but she guessed."

"She's not stupid," Sasha said.

Igor's look was wry. "That's what worries me."

Sasha laughed. "You can't have it all, Igor."

"Yes, Sasha, I can. And I will. With your help."

"Would you like me to bow, Your Majesty?"

"Not at the moment, no." He handed the bottle to his friend. "Get a message to Vlad, *da*? Set up a meeting."

"You sure he won't kick my ass just for bringing the message?"

"I think you're safe."

"You don't sound very sure."

"Vlad is the type of man that you can know for twenty years and never really *know*. Dig deep, *da*? Find out all you can about him. Childhood, lovers, how he got involved with the Ukrainians. When I meet with him, I want to be armed with information."

"And a gun?"

"Most definitely a gun. Though that might not save me if he takes offense when I ask him to kill his own leader. Vlad might just strangle me and be done with it."

"If that happens, will your father make me his successor?" Sasha asked with a teasing grin.

Igor answered with a smile and a question of his own. "Would you want that?"

Sasha tilted his head in thought. "I don't know. Do you think I'd ever be fit to be leader? I've been taking your directives for so many years I don't know if I have it in me to lead."

"I think you'd make a great leader," Igor answered truthfully. "You're loyal. To me and to our men."

"I won't ever challenge you," Sasha stated. "I trust you to do right by us."

Igor stared off into the night, gathering his thoughts. "Olaf has been acting far too long without any sort of accountability. He listens to no one. He makes unilateral decisions."

"You're just now realizing this?"

"No," Igor said. "I knew it a while ago, I just wasn't

sure what I wanted to do about it. I didn't know if I was ready to lead. I am now."

"Good."

"Promise me one thing," Igor said.

"What?"

"I don't ever want to become like my father. You're the check and balance, *da*? If I get out of control, then…"

Sasha's gaze narrowed. "Then?"

Igor stood and faced his oldest friend. "Then you'll put me down."

"I—"

"You take me down, and anyone that fights you for the role of leader. Promise me, Sasha."

Sasha swallowed. "I promise."

∽

"You smell like vodka," she murmured sleepily when Igor climbed into bed next to her.

He placed a kiss in the spot below her ear. "Sorry."

"Doesn't bother me. Just an observation." She wiggled her body against his, reached behind her to stroke his bare thigh.

He pressed closer. "How was your night?"

"Nice. I had dinner with my old roommate. It had been a while. It was nice to reconnect."

"Feel free to have her over. Anytime you want." His hands wormed their way underneath her T-shirt to settle on the warm, smooth skin of her belly.

"Thanks."

"No need to thank me. It's your home, too."

She was silent for a while, and he wondered if she'd fallen back asleep. He sincerely hoped not since he was trying to seduce her. But then she spoke.

"Isn't it weird?"

"Weird? What's weird?"

"How we got together. And that I—"

"Moved in without moving in?"

"Yeah, that."

"Do you not want to be here?"

"I want to be here," she assured him, placing her hand on his and gently scooting it lower.

He smiled into her hair as his fingers trailed below the elastic of her underwear. His smile grew wider when he caused her breath to hitch.

"You can leave anytime, Maryruth," he said huskily as he slowly grazed the most sensitive part of her. "You're not a prisoner, you're here by choice, yes?"

"Yes." She gasped. "B-b-but think of how it looks." Her last word ended on a squeak when Igor's finger slowly entered her.

He didn't know why they were wasting time talking about it—then again, women always got caught up in trivialities. All he cared about was her, in his bed, in his life. It didn't matter to him that she'd been with another man, that there had been an over-lap, or that it seemed too fast. He'd wanted her from the beginning. And now he had her —nothing was going to stop them from being together. Not even Maryruth's moot concerns.

"You want me," he breathed against her back as he slipped in a second finger. She quivered around him and let out a breathy moan. He took that as confirmation.

"I want you," he went on, pressing his erection against her.

"Is this all this is? Sex?"

"Is that what you want? Just sex?" He nipped her ear and used his thumb. She bucked against him; her body went taut and then slackened.

"I wouldn't live with a man just for sex."

He removed his hand from between her legs and gently rolled her toward him. "Then you tell me what this is."

"I'm afraid to say."

"Why?"

"Because it's too fast."

"Says who?"

She went silent.

"I've never done anything the way other people do," he said. "I've always been different that way. I spent years fighting, trying to be something I wasn't. You know what I learned? Who cares? People judge. Fuck them. You get one life. How are you going to live it?"

They faced one another, their breaths mingling, a shaft of moonlight giving them just enough light to see outlines and curves.

Maryruth rolled on top of him and stripped off her shirt. Leaning over, she grazed her lips against his. "Show me how to live, Igor."

Chapter 18

Igor told Vlad what he wanted. He didn't give him details about the *hows* and *whys*. If Vlad agreed, Igor wouldn't deign to tell him how to do it. He had a pretty good idea of how Vlad would handle it—though the man was clearly skilled in the art of hand-to-hand combat, Sasha's digging into Vlad's background revealed that he was once a Ukrainian sniper.

A wanted Ukrainian sniper.

"I do this, then you trust me, yes?" Vlad finally asked.

"If this goes off without a hitch, then I'll trust you. You'll become one of mine."

Vlad's dark eyes swam with an emotion Igor couldn't identify. It made him uncomfortable. It made him think he wasn't really the one calling the shots, but it was Vlad pulling the hidden strings.

"All right," Vlad agreed. "I'll do it. Give me three days."

Vlad rose from his chair at the table and stalked from the empty Italian restaurant. It was the only place Igor trusted to do business—the Italians—the Marinos—

weren't in his father's pocket, and the rotund, gray-haired matriarch had a soft spot for him. When her youngest son met Igor in grade school, Ori had brought Igor home to meet his family. Mama Marino had taken an instant liking to the quiet, respectful, motherless boy. The Italian mother's heart was open to any child in need.

"Here's a cannoli, on the house," Mama Marino said, placing the custard filled pastry shell in front of him.

"Thank you, Mama," Igor said, bringing her hand to his lips and giving it a kiss.

Mama Marino smiled and playfully swatted his shoulder. "You are such a flirt. If I didn't know any better, I'd think you were Italian."

Igor laughed.

"Are you still single? Gisella still talks about you."

"Gisella is married with three children," Igor pointed out with a laugh.

"Still, my daughter always had a soft spot for you."

"Like all the Marinos," Igor quipped. "You were all so good to me back then."

She gestured to the untouched cannoli. "We're good to you now. Where's your blond shadow? I haven't seen him in a while."

"Sasha." Igor smiled and cut a bite of cannoli. "He sends his love."

Mama Marino blew out a puff of air. "That one is almost as charming as you."

"I'll tell him you think so." He ate the rest of his cannoli under Mama Marino's watchful eye. Whatever the woman put in front of him, he ate, even if he was full. To leave anything on the plate was an insult.

"Who is she?" Mama Marino asked, scooping up the empty plate the moment Igor set down his fork.

"She?"

"Don't play dumb. I know there's a woman."

Igor smiled but continued to say nothing.

"She is special." It was a statement, not a question.

"Yes," Igor said.

"Good. You deserve happiness. You're such a sweet boy." She patted his cheek and then walked back into the kitchen.

Sweet boy, he thought with wry humor. He'd killed and maimed, and he just asked a Ukrainian sniper to kill the head of the Ukrainian mob to prove his loyalty.

His mother would've been *so* proud of him. The bitter thought came from deep within, but it was too late to change, too late to forge another path.

Maryruth would disagree with him. She believed people could change.

Would she come to resent him? One day down the line, would she decide that she couldn't be with a crime lord? Would she leave him?

Would he leave this life for her, if she asked?

He pondered those thoughts as he walked out into the sunny late-spring day.

She knew who he was, accepted him. Now. They were new and exciting, their banter charged with lust and young intimacy. But what happened when time marched on, the lust faded to a glowing ember, and they were left with trust, loyalty, and a life built together? A life built on his crimes.

He thought of his mother—what would've happened if she had lived? Would she have taken him away from Olaf's strangling presence? Would Igor have attended Juilliard and now be a violist?

So many wasted dreams.

Arriving home, he came into the apartment to Maryruth sitting on the floor, a pencil in hand. She looked up at him and smiled.

But to wish for a different past would mean a different future. A future that didn't include that smile.

"What are you working on?" he asked, coming over and giving her a kiss hello.

She shut what looked like a sketchbook. "Nothing." She scooped it up and held it to her chest.

"Come on, show it to me," Igor begged.

"No."

"Why not? Is it embarrassing?"

"Sort of." Her eyes dropped to the floor, her arms tightening around the sketchbook.

"I won't laugh," he promised.

Reluctantly, she released her hold on the sketchbook and handed it to him. The entire book was blank except for the last page.

"Why did you start at the back?" he asked.

"Because I hope to get better. I don't want to show off my learning mistakes."

"You drew this?"

She nodded.

"From your imagination or were you looking at something."

"Imagination."

It was only the start of a simple sketch, a gnarled tree devoid of leaves. She'd begun to tackle shading, and even though it was amateur, the promise of talent lingered on the page.

"Where did you learn to sketch?"

Maryruth bit her lip. "Auggie was teaching me."

"Why would you think this is embarrassing?" Igor asked.

She shrugged. "I don't know."

"You signed up for some college courses, didn't you?"

"Yeah."

"Any of them in art?"

Her shoulders slumped. "All of them are in art. Is that stupid? Fanciful? Hopeful?"

"It's whatever you want it to be." He handed her back the sketchbook. "It's good."

"You're just saying that."

"No. Since when have you known me to lie?"

She gave him a look and he laughed.

"Okay, I see your point. But I'm not lying about this. Does your craft need some work? Yes. But you'll get there. I have faith in you."

Her smile was slow, tentative. "You do?"

"Yes."

He had a sudden urge to play his viola, to create a piece that would mean something to her. To both of them.

Chapter 19

Maryruth and Igor spent the afternoon walking hand-in-hand through Central Park. If it weren't for Olaf's looming birthday party that evening, Igor would've been reveling in the normal moment. He would've enjoyed sharing her vanilla bean ice-cream cone. Unfortunately, the idea of introducing Maryruth to his father cast the pleasant afternoon in shadow.

"It's one night," she said. "We can get through it, don't you think?"

"I'm trying to prepare you—my father doesn't do anything half measure. I'm not even sure what's in store."

"He's having his birthday party in Atlantic City. I'm guessing gambling?"

Among other things, he didn't say. It was a black-tie event, mandatory, but that didn't mean things weren't going to get crazy later on. Olaf would expect him to participate. He had no intention of being unfaithful to Maryruth, nor did he enjoy that type of entertainment anymore.

"Hey," she said, tugging on his hand to get him to stop walking.

"Hmm?"

"Look at me. It's going to be okay."

He smiled, took her cone with his free hand, and licked. "I'm supposed to be telling you that."

"So why aren't you?"

"I don't trust my father."

"I know."

"I wish…"

"What?"

"I wish that I didn't have to get you involved in this part of my life."

"You'd prefer to have secrets from one another?"

"No. I don't know." He handed her back the ice cream and then started walking again. They rounded a curve, the green of Sheep Meadow coming into view. The park was busy today. It seemed like everyone in the city was out and about, enjoying the beautiful weather.

"I can handle your father," she said. "I got him a really nice birthday gift."

"You got him a birthday gift? You didn't have to do that."

"Let me explain to you how birthdays work."

He laughed. "What did you get him?"

"Cuff links and a bottle of vodka—a high-end bottle of vodka."

"He'll love that. Now can we stop talking about my father?"

"You brought it up," she reminded him, bringing their connected hands to her lips.

He rolled his eyes. "How's the sketch coming?"

"Good-ish. I'm not completely happy with it yet."

"Patience. You'll get there." They continued walking, dodging strollers and joggers. A bicyclist yelled he was on their right—Maryruth lunged into Igor's side in hopes of not being run over, and in the process ruined his shirt with the remainder of her ice-cream cone.

"If you didn't like my shirt, all you had to do was say something," he teased.

She laughed. "I'm sorry. And I do like your shirt."

While they were in the middle of attempting to clean up Igor's blue button down, laughing and kissing, Igor saw an animal off his leash shoot toward them, its teeth bared in an angry growl. Igor's vision narrowed as adrenaline pumped through his veins.

He yelled at Maryruth, first in Russian and then in English. He adjusted his stance, ready for the charging dog. But at the last second, the animal turned and lunged for Maryruth.

Her terrified scream rang in his ears.

Igor dove in front of Maryruth, taking the impact of the sixty-pound dog. His healing ribs ached in protest.

Man and beast fell to the ground with Igor underneath. The dog snapped its teeth at Igor's face and in self-defense, Igor shoved his forearm into the snarling jaw. He bellowed in pain. The dog growled around Igor's arm and tried to shake it like a rag doll.

His nostrils filled with the scent of blood and feral dog sweat.

Locking his legs around the animal's body, he managed to roll them both over, so that Igor pinned the dog beneath him. The beast squirmed and struggled, but even through the lancing pain, Igor shoved his arm farther into the dog's mouth. He reached into his pants pocket and pulled out a ballpoint pen he carried on him at all times.

He looked into the animal's eyes and felt no remorse as he stabbed the pen in its throat. The creature let out a pitiful whine as it choked to death on its own blood. Igor extracted his bloody arm from the dog's gaping jaws and stumbled to his feet.

Looking around, his gaze didn't settle on any of the people that gaped in silence. He only cared about one person. She stood off to the side, her face pale, her hand to her mouth. They staggered toward each other, and she threw herself into his side, not caring that he was covered in blood.

"What did you do?" a man screamed.

Igor turned, with his good arm around Maryruth, to watch the owner of the dog fall on his dead pet. He was vaguely aware of the sound of camera phones snapping pictures—no doubt someone had been recording the event.

"Your dog was about to attack my girlfriend," Igor replied, his voice cold. "He was off his leash, running through the park, and would've hurt her. Look." He held up his injured arm—he really needed to get to a hospital.

"Look what your animal did."

The man's eyes widened with shock and fear.

"I'll have your name and contact information. Now," Igor growled.

The man glanced at his fallen pet, the out-of-control beast that no one but Igor had had the balls to put down. Igor had no patience for the man's quivering lip, for the grief he was feeling at the loss of his beloved animal—an animal that he'd been unable to control.

"Fall apart later," Igor snapped. "For now, own up to your mistake. The animal should've been put down a long time ago. And you know it."

After Igor got the information he needed, he let Maryruth lead him to the street where they caught a cab bound for Lennox Hill.

"I'll be okay, *pchelka*."

"You didn't even hesitate—you just jumped in front of me. You protected me," she whispered.

He felt her tremble in his arms and brushed his lips against her hair. "I'll always protect you."

Chapter 20

Igor couldn't drink on antibiotics. *Pity*, he thought bitterly, for a bottle of vodka would have done wonders for him while he navigated Olaf's birthday party. The puncture wounds had been cleaned and covered. Minor painkillers were flowing through his veins, but the real balm to his injury was Maryruth.

She looked like Old-Hollywood glamour in a dusky pink gown with a modest neckline. An opal cameo necklace adorned her throat, and at her ears were small cameo roses. Her blonde hair was styled in a low-hanging bun that highlighted her elegant, slender neck.

Her glossy lips touched the rim of her champagne flute. Finishing off the rest of her glass, she looked at him with a sideways smile.

"Did I tell you how beautiful you look tonight?" he whispered against her ear, his hand riding low on her waist.

"Just tonight?" she teased, pressing a hand to his tuxedo jacket.

"All the nights. From now until forever."

Her smile softened, as did her gaze. "Thank you." She

looked around the private event room of the Borgata Hotel. "Your father went all out, didn't he?"

The decorations bordered on garish, but that was his father's way. Presents were stacked on the few tables in the corner. On the opposite side of the room were the bar and the chocolate and champagne fountains. This part of the evening was all business. When their colleagues' wives went to bed, the real party would begin in one of the hotel's private casinos.

"Are you ready to meet him?" Igor asked.

"Do I have a choice?"

"No."

She sighed. "I've had just enough champagne to sedate me."

"I'm jealous. I'm entirely sober. After meeting my father, I need you to drink enough for the both of us."

Maryruth laughed. "I think I can be accommodating in that regard." She slid her body close to his, letting her hand wander beneath his tuxedo jacket, her touch saying what her words didn't.

Just as Igor was about to search for his father, Sasha approached.

Like all the other men, Sasha wore a tuxedo.

"I'm surrounded by Russian James Bonds," Maryruth remarked with a smile. "You look nice, Sasha."

"Thank you," he said, with a dapper little bow, causing Igor and Maryruth to laugh. "You look beautiful."

"Thank you."

"I need to speak to you," Sasha said, turning to Igor. "It's important."

Igor looked at Maryruth.

"I'll be fine," she assured him.

"Won't be long," Igor said, pressing a quick kiss to her lips.

Dawn of an Empire

The two friends walked out of the private room and found a secluded place to talk in the lobby, a corner where they kept their voices low, their heads bent.

"It's done," Sasha said. "I have confirmation from Vlad."

Igor raised his eyebrows. "Really?"

"I've confirmed with other sources. Rostyslav is dead. Car accident," he remarked wryly. "He drove off a cliff on his way Upstate to spend time with his mistress."

"We'll meet with Vlad on Monday when we're back in the city," Igor said. Olaf's birthday celebration would last all weekend; business and pleasure would converge.

"How's she doing? How are *you* doing?"

"I'm fine. She seems... I don't know if it's really hit her yet—what happened in the park."

After Igor had been released from the hospital, he'd taken Maryruth home. She'd fallen asleep on the couch, her feet in his lap while he'd had a phone conversation with Sasha, catching him up him on the events of the afternoon.

"Good thing you always carry a ballpoint pen," Sasha remarked dryly.

Igor didn't smile. Nothing about the situation was funny. Maryruth could've been seriously injured.

He couldn't have that.

A vision of the dead dog flashed in his mind. One side of the animal had been black, the other white, a streak down the middle dividing the dueling colors. *What foreshadowing*, he thought. If only the owner had been paying attention.

He'd pay attention now. Or he'd just pay.

"What do you want to do?" Sasha asked, noting the thoughtful expression on Igor's face.

"Kill the fucker."

"Was he encouraging the animal's behavior?"

"No."

"Does he deserve it?" Sasha asked.

Igor paused. Opposing emotions raged within him. In the end, he didn't want to be Olaf; he didn't want to make poor decisions based on anger.

"All right," Igor relented.

"Let's get back to the party. I need a drink."

So did Igor, but unfortunately, sobriety was in his near future.

They headed for the ballroom. Igor wanted nothing more than to find Maryruth, wish his father a happy birthday, and then slink off to the expensive hotel suite he'd booked. He'd like nothing more than to get Maryruth into a bubble bath, watch the steam curl her blond hair, and then make love to her while the lights of Atlantic City glowed brightly through their open window. Unfortunately, his father and his injury would prevent such things from occurring.

He heard her laugh before he saw her, and when his gaze pinner her, his mouth nearly gaped. Maryruth was conversing with Olaf—and shock of all shocks, they both appeared to be enjoying each other's company.

Maryruth's eyes slid from Olaf to meet Igor's. She smiled widely. And that's when he knew that she was lying. She didn't enjoy Olaf's company, but she was giving a good show.

Igor strode purposefully toward her, wrapped his arm around her waist, and pulled her into his side. "Sorry I had to step out." To his father, he said, "Happy Birthday. I see you've met Maryruth."

Olaf's hand clenched around his drink. "Yes. Your lovely companion was kind enough to entertain me while I waited for you to greet me."

Igor refused to engage.

"This is quite a party," Sasha piped up, hoping to diffuse the tension between father and son.

"*Da*. Sonya went all out."

Sonya was Olaf's mistress of ten years. She was just as garish and greedy as he was. Some sort of loyalty kept Olaf tied to her—not that it prevented him from fooling around with other women. He was powerful, the head of the Russian mob. Not much to look at—he'd let himself go. But women still clambered over one another to get to him.

Igor wondered how it would be for him when he took over. He had no desire to be unfaithful, had no trouble believing he could be true to one woman. If the woman was Maryruth.

"Would you like to see what she bought me?" Olaf droned on, brown eyes gleaming with excitement. He didn't wait for their answers. Instead, he moved off towards the raised platform and microphone stand. In the center of the platform was an easel, a red velvet drape concealing Sonya's gift. Olaf tapped the microphone to gain everyone's attention.

The room quieted and eyes turned to Olaf. He grinned, preparing to give them a show. *He is all about the spectacle*, Igor thought snidely.

"Thank you all for coming," Olaf began. "I'm so glad to be able to spend my birthday with close friends and family."

Igor stifled his eye roll. There were easily five hundred people in the ballroom and most were business associates, or those afraid of Olaf's powerful reach. He didn't inspire loyalty—he inspired fear. And this display was nothing more than a statement of his wealth and power.

"My lovely Sonya," Olaf went on, pointing to the

woman wearing a black sequined dress that was not at all age appropriate, "has given me a beautiful painting that's too magnificent not to share with you."

Two men flanked the easel. With a nod from Olaf, they removed the red velvet curtain shielding the canvas. Olaf's eyes locked on Igor's, a satisfied smile on his face, when he revealed to five hundred people what Maryruth looked like naked.

Chapter 21

Igor's vision went red, his arm tightening around Maryruth, as if his body could shield her from Olaf's intention to embarrass them. But this was no animal he could take to the ground and kill, though Olaf was feral and malicious. The dog had just been deranged. It hadn't known any better. Olaf knew better. And he didn't give a shit.

"Igor," came Maryruth's soft whisper. "You're hurting me."

His arm slackened. She didn't move from his side. Igor didn't chance a glance at her. Instead, he kept his gaze focused on Olaf, but Olaf was too busy shaking hands and laughing with his partygoers.

"Why would he do this?" Maryruth finally asked.

"To humiliate me," Igor stated.

"I'm sorry."

He turned to look at her. Her eyes were wide, and a sheen of tears covered them.

"I've shamed you."

"No," he stated. "That painting—it's beautiful. It's raw.

It would be an honor to own such a piece."

She inhaled a shaky breath. "Then why—"

"Because Olaf wanted to put me in my place. He wanted to embarrass me in front of his colleagues, take me by surprise. No man would want his wife on display like that."

"I'm not your wife." She shook her head. "I still don't understand."

"The family business is a strange one," he began, attempting to explain. "The women are supposed to be—"

"Chaste and innocent while the men wave their infidelity and promiscuity in everyone's faces?"

"Something like that."

"Are you promiscuous?"

They were getting off topic into dangerous territory fraught with landmines. One wrong step and it would blow up in his face.

"I was," Igor admitted slowly.

"But you're not anymore?"

"Empty, it was all so empty. Do you believe me, Maryruth?"

He stared down at her, cupped her cheek in his hand. He didn't care that people stared at them, waiting for them to have an explosive fight over the unveiled painting.

"I believe you," she whispered, her breath teasing his lips. "How did he know about me? And how did he get Auggie to agree into giving him a painting?"

"I imagine a great deal of money changed hands. As for his knowing? Olaf has resources."

"Igor!" Olaf's voice thundered through the room. Voices hushed, eyes turned to the scene that was about to unfold. Olaf sauntered through the crowd to stand in front of his son. Pleasure danced in his eyes.

"Tell me, what do you think of Sonya's gift?" Olaf

taunted.

"She outdid herself," Igor said coolly.

Olaf's smile was as wide as a demonic jack-o-lantern. "Yes, she did."

"You think so?" Maryruth interjected, her voice pitched low and husky, playing into the role of an artist's muse. "That painting doesn't even hold a candle to the one I gave Igor."

Olaf's face darkened. He would not be upstaged.

Igor's arm tightened around her in a subtle warning, hoping to silence her. The last thing they needed was to arouse Olaf's vindictive nature. It was aroused enough.

"Your lover, Agoston Boros, had quite a few things to say about you," Olaf bit out. Murmured whisperers echoed in the quiet room; the showdown between the head of the Russian mob and his successor's date was too juicy not to discuss, even in the heat of the moment.

Maryruth's smile widened as she trailed a hand down the front of Igor's tuxedo jacket. "It's all true."

"Thanks for a lovely evening," Igor lied, shooting a glance at Sasha to do something—anything. "But it's best that we get going."

Olaf's fists clenched at his sides at being thwarted. Sasha jumped in front of the retreating couple and distracted Olaf by asking when the debauchery was to begin.

Igor all but dragged Maryruth by the hand through the hotel lobby.

"Slow down," she called out.

He didn't and said nothing to her until they were safely ensconced in the sleek, black Jag he'd driven to Atlantic City. The bright lights in the dark night illuminated the pavement.

"You're mad at me," she guessed, buckling her seat

belt.

Igor maneuvered through traffic like a professional racecar driver. Not taking his eyes off the road, he said, "No. But you don't realize what you've done."

"Pissed off your father? Yeah, maybe I shouldn't have had that third glass of champagne." She sighed. "I had no idea he would be like that."

"How would you have known?"

"You tried to warn me."

"*Da.*"

"But I got caught up in his charm. He seemed so…"

"I know."

She looked out the window. "I humiliated him, didn't I? In front of all those people. By not playing his game. By not being embarrassed when he tried to knock us down a few pegs."

"*Da.*" He smiled and glanced at her.

"Why are you smiling?" she demanded.

"You said 'us'."

"We are an 'us,' aren't we?"

"We are," he agreed. He cleared his throat, hating that he had to broach this subject without being able to look at her. Unfortunately, the New Jersey traffic required all of his attention.

"We have a problem," he continued.

"Yes, so you mentioned."

"There's only one way my father will leave you alone."

"Leave the city and change my name?" Maryruth quipped.

Igor paused. "A name change. Yes."

Her head whipped around, her eyes boring holes into the side of his chiseled jaw. "You can't mean what I think you mean."

"Yes, Maryruth. You have to marry me. Tonight."

Chapter 22

The car was deafeningly silent as the remains of his verbal bomb cleared the air. He heard the slight inhale of her breath. Taking his eyes off the road long enough to look at her, he watched her fingertip trail down the middle of the passenger glass window.

"All right," she said quietly. "I'll marry you."

He thought he'd feel differently. He thought he'd feel elation at achieving his heart's desire. But her words scooped out his heart like the unwanted insides of a gourd.

"There's another way," he said quietly, unable to believe what he was about to offer her.

"Yes?"

"You can leave New York. Change your name. Start over in another city."

She was silent a moment. "Without you?"

"Yes."

She was quiet again. "No."

"No?"

Dare he hope she'd choose him instead of her freedom?

"What's a life without you, Igor? I love you."

He took a hand off the wheel and searched for hers. Squeezing it, he brought it to his lips, knowing there would never be enough words to tell her how much he loved her, how much he needed her.

"I love you, Maryruth. And I'll spend the rest of my life showing you."

It was her turn to bring his hand to her lips. "I look forward to it."

He laughed, feeling lighter than he had in years. And then he made a call that would change their lives forever.

When they arrived at the airstrip, he helped Maryruth out of the Jag and ushered her toward the private runway. Once they were seated and buckled in the small plane, Maryruth asked, "Vegas?"

He smiled but shook his head.

"Tell me," she said with a laugh.

"Vermont."

"Why Vermont?" she asked.

"Because I hate Elvis," he quipped.

She laughed again, held his gaze. "Are we doing this? For real?"

He raised an eyebrow. "As opposed to? This is serious to me. This is for life."

"Life," she breathed.

"Yours and mine."

She nodded. "Yours and mine."

∽

The couple that owned the bed and breakfast didn't balk at Igor's demanding tone, and when he threw more than enough money to buy out the entire inn for the weekend, their demeanors changed from merely accommodating to downright obsequious.

They summoned the justice of the peace, and by the light of the full moon, Igor and Maryruth were married in the garden, among blooming roses and fireflies.

Igor kissed his new bride softly, with the promise of a beautiful life to come. He couldn't wait to plan their future —there was so much they hadn't yet discussed. He didn't care if they disagreed about politics, religion, or money. None of that mattered because they both had money, and with money, they could solve anything.

After a quick champagne toast with the owners and justice of the peace, Igor asked Maryruth to sit in the parlor and wait for him to come for her.

Trust and love burned in her eyes.

Thirty minutes later, Igor returned and gently lifted a sleepy Maryruth into his arms. He inhaled sharply at the pain in his injured arm.

"I can walk," she protested.

He refused to let her down despite the discomfort. "I thought it was tradition to carry the bride across the threshold," he teased, feeling a bit delirious.

"It's not our threshold," she reminded him as he made his way up the dimly lit staircase to the largest suite.

"We should talk about that."

"About what?" she asked, lifting her head from his chest.

"What kind of threshold you want."

They arrived at their room, and Igor managed to fiddle with the knob.

The glow of soft candlelight turned the room gold. The king-sized bed with a white, antique lace coverlet was dusted with red rose petals.

"Oh," she breathed.

He gently released her. "I told you I'd turn you into a rose petals and candlelight woman."

She smiled and reached out to caress his jaw. "Thank you. This has been—I couldn't have—thank you."

"You don't have any regrets?" He shut the door and stripped off his coat, throwing the jacket on a nearby chair.

"About?"

"So many things."

She began pulling pins out of her hair. Dark-blond tresses cascaded down her back. She enchanted him; he couldn't look away.

"I don't have a ring to give you," he said.

"And when has a ring ever meant anything?" she asked, slowly stalking towards him as she began removing her jewelry.

"Your parents didn't come to our wedding. Does that bother you?"

"I don't speak to my parents," she reminded him, her hands reaching for the zipper that she'd never be able to undo without his help.

"I'm not enough for you," he whispered.

Turning, she presented her back and looked at him over her shoulder. "You're everything, Igor. When will you believe that?"

He didn't answer as he grasped her zipper and slowly tugged it down to reveal her smooth, bare back. *Will you love me, even through my darkness?* He didn't ask. Tonight, their wedding night, was not for his confessions and fears. Tonight, their wedding night, was just for them.

The chiffon dress pooled at her feet. She left her heels on, a blend of siren and innocence, all wrapped up in one beautiful, unique package. He'd known she was different from the first moment they spoke all those months ago at the bathhouse. He just hadn't realized she was also his salvation, his reason for wanting to be a better man. He might fail at that, but he couldn't help but try.

"You're my wife," he breathed, his hands caressing skin and curves.

"You're my husband. And you're still in your clothes."

He let her strip him bare and then guided her to bed. He refused to let her be anything but a beautiful, cherished prize he didn't deserve.

When she was primed and ready for him, begging, achy and needy, he loomed over her and whispered, "Your smell, your taste, I want to bury myself in you."

She locked her legs around him, urging him closer, arching her back so they were skin to skin. "Yeah? What are you waiting for?"

Chapter 23

Igor awoke the next morning with a burst of energy, even though they hadn't gone to sleep until dawn, not until the candles burned out and the rose petals were nothing more than fragrant reminders of what had transpired between them.

He left her tousled, sated, and asleep. Igor's steps were light as he walked the sleepy Vermont town's cobblestone streets. No one had stirred yet, but with the aid of the bed and breakfast owners, he was able to find the one and only coffee shop as well as the antique jewelry store.

Half an hour later, he had everything he needed. Igor wasn't one to waste time—when he saw perfection, he knew it.

Heading back to the coffee shop for his second cup, he bought two breakfast sandwiches and one of every kind of baked good.

"I just got married," Igor said to the counter girl, wanting to share his good fortune.

The young brunette smiled. "Congratulations." When he tried to pay, she waved him away. "On the house."

He left her a one-hundred-dollar tip.

The morning was bright and warm as Igor made his way back to the bed and breakfast. Maryruth was still asleep, sprawled out in the center of the bed. He set the coffee and bags down on the bedside table before kissing her shoulder blade.

"Igor?" she whispered.

He kissed her lips, his tongue dipping into her mouth. Soon, she was kissing him back. He quickly stripped out of his clothes before climbing into bed. Rolling on top of his wife, he gently nudged her legs open and slipped inside.

She gasped and moaned, clawed and scraped his back. Maryruth kept her eyes closed even when he quickened the pace, even as she shattered around him. Holding her, their breaths settled.

The late morning light filtered into the room, reminding him they couldn't stay there forever—no matter how much he wanted to. If only they were simple beasts; life would've been nothing except rutting, eating, and sleeping. But they were human, and with that came obligations and worries.

"Good morning," she whispered, finally opening her eyes as she snuggled against his warm chest.

"Sleep well?" he asked.

"Hmm. No. Not at all." She smiled against the column of his neck and pressed a kiss there.

"You don't seem too upset."

"I'm not. Last night was the best night of my life. You've set the bar really high," she teased. "Do I smell coffee?"

"And scones and a breakfast sandwich."

He sat up and reached for the bags, setting them in front of her. He watched as she peeked in each one, smiling to himself when she stilled.

"This isn't food," she remarked, her voice faint, as she gestured to a small, white bag with gold scrawl stamped across the front.

"It's not?" he asked, eyes widening in sham innocence. "Hmm. I wonder what it could be."

She bit her lip and hesitantly reached into the bag and pulled out a small black ring box.

"Why are you waiting? Open it. It's yours."

"Women, all women, even women who aren't romantic, always dream of the piece of jewelry they hope to find in this type of box." She gazed at the ring container like it was a serpent ready to strike.

"Open it," he urged again. Most men would be afraid of the unknown reaction waiting for them. He was not most men. When he saw the ring, he knew it belonged to her.

She flipped the box open. There, nestled on a canvas of black, was a platinum rose cut diamond ring. Sunlight filtered through the room, shooting rainbow prisms across the far wall.

"Oh." She breathed. A lone tear gathered at the corner of her eye before falling as gently as a snowflake.

"May I?" he asked, his voice filled with reverence for this woman, this ring, this moment.

Unable to speak, Maryruth nodded and held out her slender hand. The ring fit perfectly. Igor brought it to his lips and kissed it before turning over her hand and kissing her palm.

Her newly adorned hand reached out to touch his cheek. "Where's your ring?" she asked quietly.

"I picked your ring. I think it's only fair for you to choose mine."

And with that statement, he watched Maryruth finally lose control as she cried tears of joy.

Chapter 24

After they'd eaten and had a steamy romp in the shower, they'd reluctantly got moving. They had made a quick stop at the antique jewelry store and Maryruth picked out a simple, classic band for Igor.

Igor had left Sasha a message, apprising him of the situation and asking him to reach out to Vlad for an immediate meeting. Igor's timeline needed to be moved up. He was done playing Olaf's games. He was ready to take what was his, lead, live.

Love.

He looked over at the woman who had changed everything for him.

She caught his look, shot him a crooked smile, settled in her airplane seat, and closed her eyes. They were flying back to Atlantic City to grab Igor's car, and then they'd drive back to New York.

Maryruth opened her eyes and glanced at her ring finger as she asked the question that was plaguing both of them. "Will your father accept me?"

"He has no choice."

She sighed. "Not exactly what I wanted to hear. I wish your father didn't have that painting of me," she said sleepily, her eyes drifting shut again.

"He won't have it for long."

"You plan on buying it from him?"

"No," Igor stated. "There's not enough money in the world that would get my father to part with it. He wants to torment me with it."

"Then how do you plan to get it if you can't buy it?"

"Steal it, of course."

"Of course," she murmured, her smile slipping as she fell asleep.

She slept the entire plane ride, but Igor remained awake. His mind churned. He thought of scenarios, made a mental list of all that needed to be dealt with the moment he was back in New York.

Even before he met with his father, he needed to see Sasha and Vlad. Igor wanted a pulse on the Ukrainian situation. They might still be in turmoil over the sudden loss of their leader, but Vlad would know better than Igor if the Ukrainians were ready for a sit-down. And when the time came, he would have Vlad on his left, Sasha on his right.

Hope stirred in his chest when he looked at a sleeping Maryruth. He gently touched her shoulder and brushed his lips across her forehead.

She snuggled into him. "We there yet?" she murmured sleepily.

"Not yet. Landing soon."

Covering her mouth, she didn't bother stifling a yawn. "I can't wait to get home and change."

They were still in their wrinkled formalwear.

He cleared his throat. "Where would you like to go?" he asked, taking her hand.

"Go? Go where?" She leaned her head against his shoulder.

"Our honeymoon."

"Honeymoon?"

"You've heard of a honeymoon, yes?"

She snorted with laughter. "Yes, I know what a honeymoon is. Is now a good time for it?"

"Why do you ask?"

Lifting her head, she looked at him. "When I was speaking to your father, he implied…"

"Go on," he urged.

"That you were about to become very busy."

Igor's pulse pounded in his ears, but he forced himself to remain calm.

"He said he was," she used air quotes, "'grooming you'. To take over the family business."

The knots in his belly unraveled. "He's been grooming me for years. He's completely unsatisfied with who I am as a person."

"You sound remarkably cheerful," she said dryly.

Igor shrugged. "I'm no longer a child—I've learned there's no pleasing him. Why try?"

She sighed. "Yeah, I've been there."

"When did you stop trying to please your parents?"

"Subconsciously? About sixteen. Consciously—eighteen. When I moved to New York."

They began their descent into Atlantic City. Maryruth opened the sliding window slat and peered out at the encroaching landscape. "I wish I could've met her."

"Who, *pchelka*?"

"Your mother." She looked at him and smiled. "It would've been nice to meet the woman solely responsible for keeping you intact."

He smiled softly and kissed her lips.

"Be careful, Igor," she said, worry pervading her eyes. "I don't trust Olaf."

"One step ahead of you. I haven't trusted him for years." He tugged her close and wrapped an arm around her. "Don't worry about him. Worry about where we should take our honeymoon."

A few hours later, they were home. Maryruth kicked off her heels in the foyer and dashed towards the bedroom and called, "Shower time!"

He grinned. "I'll join you in a bit."

She blew him a kiss and disappeared. He waited a few minutes to ensure he had privacy before calling Sasha.

"Ah, the married man has resurfaced," Sasha teased.

Igor smiled into the phone. "Barely."

"I've been waiting years to throw you a *malchishnik*. And then you eloped. I'll never get a chance now."

"Sorry."

"You're not sorry at all," Sasha pointed out.

"No, not in the least."

Igor wouldn't have changed his wedding for anything in the world. Just the two of them, a few witnesses, under the light of the full moon. Intimate, quiet, private. Just what he liked.

"We need to talk about business," Igor stated, steering the conversation into the direction it needed to go. "Mama Marino's. Tomorrow."

"Am I calling Vlad, or are you?" Sasha asked.

"I will. The man has earned the right to hear from me personally."

"*Da*, he has. What about Olaf? He's been calling my phone non-stop."

"Are you answering?"

"Yes. Those first few phone calls were nothing but drunken rants."

"Did I ruin his birthday?" Igor asked with a smile in his voice.

"Completely."

"Glad to hear it."

"Igor!" Maryruth called.

All thoughts of his angry father slipped away when he thought of his wet and naked wife waiting for him in the shower.

"Have to go," he said to Sasha. "Tomorrow, eight a.m.—Mama Marino's."

Igor hung up, tossed his phone onto the couch, and stalked towards the bedroom, removing his clothes as he went. The bathroom was already filled with steam.

"Coming in," he said, so as not to startle her. He opened the glass door of the shower and quickly shut it, trapping the heat.

Maryruth turned and smiled. She looked like a mermaid with her blond hair covering her breasts, her blue eyes gleaming with desire.

She gently pushed him against the wall. "Took you long enough."

Her hand stroked him and he gritted out, "Won't take me long at all. Not if you keep doing what you're doing."

Laughing, her grip tightened. Her other hand stroked up and down his side, slid up his back to rest at the base of his neck. "Kiss me," she whispered.

He obliged, tilting his head down to capture her lips. He pushed his erection deeper into her hand, but it wasn't enough. Growling into her mouth, he pushed away from the wall and maneuvered her up against it.

"My turn," he whispered huskily.

She dropped her hand and lifted a leg.

His fingers and tongue seemed to be everywhere, all at once, tasting, demanding, needing. Then, he was entering her, slowly, inch by inch, until she was sucking in air.

When he was hilt deep, he grasped her head and stared into her eyes. He wanted to watch as he pleasured her.

"Igor," she whispered.

Her pleas and moans made him feel like a man. She owned him.

He'd never been happier.

Chapter 25

Sasha looked at his watch and let out a sigh. "He's late."

"I know," Igor replied, taking a bite of the spinach and mushroom frittata.

"Why aren't you upset about it? You gave him a chance to prove himself—he followed through—and now he's late. Is this some sort of power play? To prove he'll come when he wants and that he won't be summoned?"

Igor paused thoughtfully. "Maybe." He lifted his espresso cup to his lips and finished the shot. It hadn't been sitting more than a minute and it had already turned bitter. Espresso had a very short life.

Sasha glanced at him, his high cheekbones fused with pink. "How can you be so calm about this? What am I missing?"

Igor was spared from answering by the arrival of Vlad. He stalked silently through the empty restaurant, black sunglasses shielding his eyes. He took them off, rested them on the table, and then pulled out his chair.

"My sincerest apologies about being late," Vlad said.

His tone and stance were dutifully contrite, but there was something he wasn't saying.

"You couldn't call?" Sasha demanded, letting his temper get the best of him.

Vlad raised a dark eyebrow. "Do I report to you now?"

"No," Igor interrupted. "You report to me."

Vlad sighed. "I know this. I thought to tell you in person what I've been dealing with this weekend while you were in Atlantic City."

Igor didn't volunteer that he'd only been in AC for a night. Igor owed no one an explanation.

"The Bosnians and Chechens are encroaching on Ukrainian territory."

"What Ukrainian territory?" Sasha asked.

"What's left of it," Vlad stated, not rising to Sasha's bait.

The two of them needed a fight in The Arena where they could settle who had the bigger *khuy*.

"If you want Ukrainian territory, Ukrainian force, then you need to step in. Now." Vlad's dark eyes searched Igor's face. "That's what this was about for you—all along. Mercenaries. Ukrainian mercenaries."

Igor neither confirmed nor denied it. "Have you spoken with your people?"

"Yes. If the Bosnians and Chechens have their way, there won't be anything left of the Ukrainian mob in New York."

"The Ukrainian mob won't exist as they know it if I lead," Igor pointed out. "They'll swear fealty to me."

"Yes. But in exchange, you promise them safety, prosperity, and a chance. We don't have that now. We don't have a direction. We're soldiers without a leader."

Igor waited, churning over the words in his mind. "We will destroy the Bosnians and Chechens."

"In exchange for?" Vlad pressed. The man wasn't stupid. He might've been a soldier who preferred missions to leadership, but he wasn't stupid.

"In exchange for removing Olaf Dolinsky as the head of the Russian mafia."

It was the first time Igor had spoken out loud to someone other than Sasha about the end result he wanted to achieve.

Vlad held out his hand and Igor clasped it. The two men shook.

Business, for the moment, concluded, the three of them sat back and enjoyed their breakfast.

"I suppose congratulations are in order, yes?" Vlad stated.

"Premature, don't you think?" Igor asked. "I'm not leader of anything yet."

Vlad's eyes dipped to the wedding band on Igor's ring finger.

"Ah, yes. I was married over the weekend."

"*Pazdraviyayoo.*"

Igor inclined his head.

Mama Marino came out of the kitchen, brandishing a wooden spoon, a spotless red and white checkered apron covering her ample form.

She looked at the plate in front of Vlad. "You did not finish your meal."

"Your food is delicious, but I ate before I came."

Mama Marino stared Vlad down, her brown eyes trained on his face.

Igor held his breath.

Mama Marino smacked the top of Vlad's head with her wooden spoon. He cursed violently in Ukrainian. She smacked him again.

"I have only two rules: you finish whatever I place in front of you, and no cursing. Not in any language."

Wincing, Vlad rubbed his head, but nodded, looking like a chastised choirboy. "My deepest apologies. I will clean my plate."

"It's lunch time," she stated. "I'll bring you more food."

Vlad waited until Mama Marino had disappeared into the kitchen before leaning over the table and whispering, "She's trying to kill me—with food."

"It's the best way to go," Igor assured him.

"You could've warned me," Vlad muttered.

Igor laughed. "Where's the fun in that?"

Mama Marino returned with three plates of branzini, sautéed escarole, and a polenta dish. She placed the food in front of the three strapping men, put her hands on her hips, and waited. Vlad picked up his fork and shoveled in a bite, smiling around a mouthful of green leaves.

Igor reached for his glass of water and took a sip.

"What's this?" Mama Marino said, lifting Igor's hand and examining his ring.

"I got married. Over the weekend," Igor explained, refusing to squirm, though Mama Marino's gaze made him want to.

"I was not invited?"

"We eloped."

"I have not met her."

"You will."

"When?" she demanded. "Today."

"Not today."

"Tomorrow then. Night." Her brown gaze was steely.

"I have to check our schedules."

"Tomorrow night," she reiterated.

He sighed. "Tomorrow night."

"Promise."

"Promise."

"Does she like Italian food?"

"Loves it," Igor claimed even though he had no idea.

She pointed her finger at him. "Tomorrow night."

He nodded.

Mama Marino retreated and Igor let out a breath. Vlad and Sasha laughed at him and Igor joined in. "No one is safe from the wrath of Mama Marino."

"I heard that!" yelled Mama Marino's voice through the kitchen door.

Chapter 26

After leaving Sasha and Vlad, Igor took a cab to his father's penthouse apartment on the Upper East Side. After the death of Igor's mother, Olaf had moved from Brooklyn to the UES. Igor hated the area. Old money reigned, and Igor never understood why his father would choose to live among those that had done nothing to deserve their wealth, only inherited it.

Igor preferred Battery Park, and though he owned his apartment, he'd earned it. He was in line to lead the Russian mob, but he'd spent years working as nothing more than a lowly foot soldier, a minion. Igor had secured his spot as Olaf's second.

He greeted his father's doorman and then headed toward the elevators but was stopped. Apparently, Igor had to be announced now. He used to be able to come and go as he pleased.

Another one of Olaf's moves to prove who was in power. Not for long. Igor waited thirty minutes before his father deigned to let him up.

When he walked into his father's penthouse, he was

immediately greeted by the nude painting of Maryruth. It was the first thing guests saw upon arrival.

A wave of possessive jealousy tore through him. He'd made his peace with Maryruth's past, including the time she was with Agoston Boros, but this—this he would not make peace with.

His father sat on the couch, flipping through the newspaper, pretending he didn't derive a sick satisfaction from his son's torment.

Igor locked that shit down and quickly.

"Gorgeous painting," Igor remarked blandly, taking a moment to really study it. Installed behind museum glass, there was no glare. The sunlight filtering through the windows highlighted the bright colors and curves of Maryruth's body.

It belonged in an exhibit. It was meant to be fawned over. Not held as some power play.

Olaf looked up at the painting, a slight smirk skipping about his lips. "I think so. Well worth the price."

He wasn't talking about money and Igor knew it.

"How much to buy it from you?" Igor asked even though he knew his father would never part with it. Not while he was alive.

"It's not for sale."

"Shame," Igor said as he sat on the opposite couch from his father. "It would've made the perfect wedding gift to Maryruth."

Olaf frowned. "Wedding gift? You're getting married?"

Igor smiled and held up his left hand. "Married. Just this past weekend." It was Igor's turn to feel a glimmer of satisfaction when he heard Olaf's jaw clench and his teeth grind.

"What?" Igor asked, pretending to flick a piece of lint

off of his gray suit pants. "You're not going to offer me your felicitations?"

"You married her," Olaf stated through a tight throat. "Why? Just to piss me off?"

Igor laughed. "That was just a byproduct."

Olaf scoffed. "You think you love her."

Igor's eyes narrowed. "What do you know about love?"

"You want to talk about *her*." He sneered.

"You never want to talk about her."

"She's dead. What's there to talk about?"

Igor shook his head. "God, I pity you."

"Don't. I don't need your pity." He waved his hand, gesturing to the expansive living room of the Upper East Side apartment. There was nothing subtle about garish opulence. "Look what I have built."

How many had to die so you could dine on caviar and champagne? How many more will die before your reign comes to an end? Igor didn't ask. His father had always been delusional.

The door to the apartment opened. Cloying perfume permeated the air. The rustle of designer tissue paper in shopping bags alerted Igor to his father's mistress. Today she wore a low-cut white shirt. He wasn't even offended, just sad for her.

"Igor!" she exclaimed with false cheer, setting her acquisitions down in the corner for the housekeeper to tend to. "I didn't know you'd be here."

"He was just leaving," Olaf stated.

Igor rose and stared his father in the eye. "You will accept her."

The tacit threat hung in the air. At this stage, neither man wanted to test the will of the other.

Olaf nodded once.

Igor passed Sonya, holding his breath as he went.

The scents in his home differed greatly from his father's house. He closed his eyes and leaned against the door, inhaling the aroma of clean air wafting through the open windows. He'd always loved summer in New York. Now, more so than ever.

Maryruth sat at the kitchen table, blond head bent over a stack of paperwork. Ear buds were jammed into her ears and plugged into an iPod that rested next to her. She set down the pen and rubbed her wrist. Turning, she started when she saw him standing quietly behind her. She yanked out her ear buds and glared at him.

"What the hell? You scared me." She pressed a hand to her heart. "I didn't hear you come in."

"Sorry," he said, not making a move toward her. He was afraid if he went to her, he'd claim her mouth, her body. Use her to unleash all his anger at his father onto her—and she didn't deserve that. She'd take it because she loved him.

He needed to find a way to calm his own beast.

She cocked her head to one side. "You okay?"

He thought about it a moment and then shook his head.

She patted the chair next to her. "Tell me."

Igor didn't hesitate. The chair scraped across the floor as he pulled it out and sat. His hand reaching out to gently squeeze her thigh.

"Hi," he whispered, leaning in.

Her hand came up to stroke his cheek as she leaned in to kiss him. Sunlight caught the magnificent diamond on her finger, reminding him of everything that truly mattered.

"Met with my father," he stated gruffly when his lips reluctantly left hers.

"Ah. Don't tell me what he said."

"He said—"

"No, I'm serious." Her eyes were open, guileless. "I don't want to know because I don't care." She gestured to the stack of papers. "Look what I'm doing."

A small smile appeared on his lips when he realized what she was taking care of.

"Fucking bureaucracy," she muttered with an eye roll. "Do you know how much effort and time it takes to legally change your name?"

"Perhaps then you'll never threaten to divorce me," he teased. "Paperwork is a nightmare."

She laughed. "I don't plan on divorce."

"No?" he asked quietly.

Maryruth stood and picked up her empty coffee mug. Bending over, she kissed him on the lips. "No. Not at this time. Get back to me at the seven-year mark. I hear it itches."

They laughed together. It was a balm to Igor's heart. He was back to pitying his father.

"Tea?" she asked, holding the silver teakettle under the faucet.

"Please." His eyes roved over the stack of papers on top of her sketchbook. Just enough of the corner peeked out to intrigue him.

"Go ahead," she said.

It was his turn to start. "You don't mind?"

She leaned against the counter and crossed her ankles. "No. I don't mind."

He pulled out the sketchbook to reveal the drawing on the page. "It looks like a garden. A rose garden."

"It is. It's my vision for the roof. It's a great space up

there. But there's nothing except a few chairs and a great view. I thought a rooftop garden would be nice."

Igor looked at her, really looked at her like he was seeing her for the first time. "I love you. Did you know that?"

She smiled in happiness. "I'm glad. Because you," she uncrossed her ankles and sauntered to him, "Igor Dolinsky, are stuck with me. Forever."

He pulled her onto his lap and pressed his head to her heart. "It's because you hate paperwork, right? That's the only reason?"

Igor felt a rumble against his ear.

"Yes."

"Glad we have that established."

"Igor?"

"Hmmm?"

She gently tugged on his hair to get him to look at her. "I love you, too. Forget the tea. Take me to bed."

Chapter 27

The old brick walls of Mama Marino's restaurant were graced with black and white photos of generations of Marinos, along with antique cooking utensils. It was warm, inviting. Customers felt like they were stepping into an Italian home at the turn of the century. It was part of Mama Marino's unique charm.

"This is lovely," Maryruth stated, looking around as Igor helped her with her chair. "And it smells delicious. What is that?" She sniffed the air. "Lamb, I think?"

"Good nose," Igor said with a smile before taking his own seat.

They weren't seated for two minutes before a silent waiter arrived at their table and poured them a bottle of something red. When he disappeared into the kitchen, Maryruth leaned over and whispered, "Did you set that up in advance?"

Igor shook his head. "Mama will give you what she wants to give you. Best to go with it, *pchelka*."

Maryruth shrugged and smiled, picking up the glass of

wine and sniffing its contents. She took a tiny sip before setting it back down. "Mama has good taste."

Mama Marino came out of the kitchen with the first course: plates of antipasti, meats, olives, cheese, and hot, steaming bread right from the oven. She plopped everything down onto the table with a great flourish. Then, she yanked Igor from his seat and embraced him. Next, she turned her laser-focused, brown gaze onto Maryruth.

"You," Mama stated.

"Me," Maryruth chimed.

"Stand. So I can hug you."

Igor stifled a laugh as he watched Maryruth nearly disappear into Mama Marino's ample chest. "Sit," Mama Marino commanded. "Eat."

"Thank you," Maryruth murmured, looking dazed as she placed the white cloth napkin in her lap.

"You try the wine?"

Maryruth nodded. "Incredible."

"From one of our vineyards. In Italy."

"Thank you, Mama."

"Someone wants to say hello." She turned her head toward the kitchen and bellowed in Italian. A moment later, a man with dark brown curls came through the double door, wiping his hand on his white apron.

"Ori!" Igor shouted, jumping up and embracing the man.

"Igor," the booming Italian greeted, slapping Igor on the back. Ori's eyes darted to Maryruth. "You must be the wife."

Maryruth stood up again, the napkin in her lap falling to the floor. "Maryruth. Nice to meet you."

Ori clasped her hand and hauled her against him. She let out a surprised *oof* causing everyone, even Mama Marino, to laugh.

"Sit and eat," Ori stated. He waited for Igor to sit before placing his hand on his shoulder, leaning in and whispering, "We'll speak later?"

Igor glanced at Maryruth who was watching their exchange. He nodded.

"More food comes out in fifteen minutes," Mama Marino warned.

"We'll be ready," Igor assured her.

The Marinos left them to eat. Igor picked up the serving spoon and held it out to her. She took it but didn't make a move to serve herself. "What was that about?" she asked.

"What?"

"That moment with Ori?"

Igor hesitated a moment before replying. "He's going to help me with some business."

She took a deep breath. "Okay."

He raised an eyebrow. "Okay? You're not going to demand specifics?"

"What good would that do?" she asked in honest curiosity.

Igor took her hand, skimmed his thumb over her knuckles. "You really do trust me, don't you?"

She cocked her head to one side and grinned. "Isn't that one of the pillars?"

"Pillars?"

"Of a solid marriage."

He laughed. "We've been married three days."

"We're nailing it, this marriage thing," she quipped. "Now eat your *capicola* before Mama Marino takes your head off."

"You know what *capicola* is? I'm impressed."

"Google."

"Ah," he said, dropping her hand.

As she served him and then herself, Igor's cell phone buzzed in his pocket. "Have to take this," he said, rising from his chair and looking at the screen.

"I'll be here. Trying to make a dent in all this food."

He laughed as he stalked out of the restaurant. Rounding the corner into the alley, he answered his phone to speak to Vlad. It was a quick conversation. Everything was ready to go on his end. Igor would have the rest ironed out by the end of the evening—after he spoke with Ori. Igor went back inside, but before returning to Maryruth, he diverged and headed to the bathroom. When he was finished, he opened the door and nearly collided with Mama Marino who was waiting for him.

"Yes?" Igor asked with a slight smile. "Can I help you with something?"

Mama Marino stared up at him, her arms crossed over her chest. She was silent. He waited.

"Your wife..."

Igor raised an eyebrow.

"She's keeping something from you."

"How do you—"

"Because I raised three girls. I know when they're hiding something. And that one"—she pointed in the direction of Maryruth— "is hiding something."

She patted his cheek before disappearing back into the domain of her kitchen. Igor took a moment to compose himself and then went to the table. Maryruth looked up at him with the fork in her mouth.

"Everything okay?" she asked.

He nodded, placing the napkin in his lap.

"Bad news?" she pressed.

"Everything is fine."

A crease formed between Maryruth's brows. "You're acting funny."

"Am I?" Igor reached for his glass of wine and then downed a hefty swallow.

"Yes. You were fine before the phone call. Therefore, it's safe to conclude that the phone call is the reason for your change in attitude. And why you're snapping at me."

He trusted Mama Marino's instincts. She'd been the sole maternal figure in his life after the death of his mother. Along with raising three daughters, she'd also raised three sons, all of whom were involved in the Italian family business. Why would she lie?

"Want to tell me something?" Igor purred.

"Tell you what?" Her voice was calm, but he saw the rapid flicker of her pulse at her neck.

"Maryruth," he warned.

"Why don't you tell *me* what you want me to tell you? Because you obviously think I have something to tell you," she babbled. "And don't take that tone with me."

His jaw gaped. "What tone?"

"That tone that says you're disappointed in me for something I did or didn't do."

"Did you do something?" His heart tightened. Had she betrayed him in some way? Was his world about to come crashing to the ground?

"Do something?" she repeated flatly. "I didn't do it alone."

He frowned in confusion. "Do what alone?"

She sighed. "Pregnant. I'm pregnant, Igor."

Chapter 28

"How?" he asked, feeling like he was about to pass out.

She snorted. "The usual way. Sperm meets egg and then—"

He held up his hand. "I don't need a biology lesson. When did you find out?"

"Doctor confirmed it a few days ago."

"And you waited to tell me!" he roared.

Other patrons of the restaurant turned their heads to stare. Mama Marino dashed out of the kitchen, looking around for the source of the noise. When she realized it was Igor, her shoulders sank and her spine relaxed.

"Can we not do this—here?" Maryruth pleaded.

"What's happening?" Mama Marino asked.

Maryruth glared at her. "This doesn't concern you."

"It concerns me," Mama Marino snapped back. "If it concerns his well-being. What did you do to him?"

"Me?" Maryruth stood and went nose to nose with Mama Marino. "Your precious Igor knocked me up. That's what happened!"

Someone cleared a throat. The three of them realized

the restaurant was completely silent, and then Ori's booming laugh came from the doorway of the kitchen. "Limoncello for everyone! On the house!"

Conversation began again.

Igor had never seen Mama Marino speechless. The woman recovered and then hauled Maryruth against her to whisper something in her ear. Maryruth nodded and closed her eyes, leaning into the woman's motherly embrace.

Shame flooded him. The woman of his dreams, his *wife*, had just told him she was pregnant with their child, and he'd yelled at her. Yelled at her in public for keeping it to herself.

"You two," Mama Marino said. "In the kitchen. Now."

Maryruth went first, followed by Igor. Mama Marino brought up the end. "Open another few bottles of Limoncello!" she called to Ori.

"Okay, Mama," he replied with a grin, and then went back to pouring out shot glasses of the sweet, yellow liqueur.

When they got to the kitchen, Mama Marino barked in Italian. The kitchen emptied. "Talk," she said to Igor and Maryruth. "No yelling. Not good for the bambino."

The woman left.

Maryruth faced him. "I didn't tell you right away because I needed to be sure and I took a moment, you know? Where it was just about me and processing—"

"Stop. I'm a *mudak*. This is not on you." He didn't make a move to touch her. "Mama Marino said you were keeping something from me."

"How did she know?" Maryruth asked in amazement.

"She didn't know what you were keeping to yourself, only that there was something you weren't sharing with me."

"So we should blame Mama for all of this?"

"Maybe. Doesn't excuse my reaction. Or that I yelled at you."

She stared at him with wide eyes. "Why did you? Yell, I mean?"

"Shock, surprise." He paused. "Fear."

"Fear? About me?"

He shook his head. "You've met my father."

"Yes." She nodded. "Oh. Oh, I see."

"What if—"

"No."

"But—"

"*No.*" She was the one who moved to him, pressing her body close to his. "It will never be like that. You're not like that. Not like him."

He crushed her to him and closed his eyes. "When did this happen?"

"Honestly? I think it happened the first night we were together."

"At The Arena?"

She nodded against him.

"That was a hot night," he stated.

She laughed. "Yeah. It was."

"How do you feel about it?"

Leaning back, she stared up at him, all the love she had for him shining out through her blue eyes. "Happy."

He smiled softly. "Happy?"

"Elated. Joyful." Her smile slipped. "You? Are you thinking that I did this on purpose?"

"No." His hands moved from around her to cradle her cheeks. "No. For whatever reason. This happened. We happened."

"But are you happy about it, Igor?"

The shock was fading. He examined the feeling welling within him. "No, Maryruth. I'm not happy."

Her face fell. "Oh."

"I'm grateful. So fucking grateful."

Maryruth smiled and sighed. "Oh."

Igor's lips covered hers for a brief moment. "Will you give me a moment—I have to speak to Ori. It can't wait."

She nodded.

"It will be fast. Then we'll go home. And celebrate. The way we're supposed to."

She sighed again. "Celebrate."

◦∼◦

Igor rolled over, stroking a hand down Maryruth's bare back. "Are you awake?"

She mumbled.

"Maryruth," he urged.

"What?"

"Wake up, I want to talk to you."

"About what?" She didn't move from her position on her stomach, but she did flip her head to face him.

"I think we should move out of the city."

"Okay, can't this wait until morning? I need my sleep."

He laughed. "Please?"

She sighed and flopped onto her back. "Okay. I'm awake. Talk."

"I think moving out of the city is a good idea."

"I don't."

"Why not?"

"Nothing has changed, Igor."

"Everything has changed."

"I like the city. I like this apartment. I like the idea of

planting a rooftop garden. I don't want everything to change just because we're having a baby."

"But everything is changing. Has changed. Will continue to change."

"Igor—"

"What about me?" he demanded. "I want to protect you and our—" He couldn't even say it, not yet. He was still in shock. "But I also need this for me. Things are about to change with the business. Become more dangerous. So I'm asking, Maryruth. For me."

She sighed. "All right, Igor. All right."

"Thank you, *pchelka*." He searched for her lips and found them. They lingered for a moment before pulling back. He rolled onto his back, and she scooted her way across the bed and curled into him. His hand sank into her hair, and he began to stroke her scalp. She made a noise very much like a purr.

"Can I ask you something?" he whispered.

"Uh-hmm."

"Why aren't you more in shock? About the baby?"

She was quiet while her fingers trailed swirls across his thigh. "My childhood was stifling. For any kid, but especially for a kid like me. I wanted to learn, and travel, and experience *life*. But I just couldn't. Not in that house. Not with them."

Maryruth stopped talking, but Igor knew she wasn't done. So he waited.

"There was only a five percent chance," she said so softly he wasn't sure he heard her.

"Five percent chance for what?" he asked.

"That I'd even be able to get pregnant. I have endometriosis, Igor. I didn't tell you I was pregnant right away because I needed the doctor to ensure it wasn't ectopic. I wanted to know for sure before I—well, before I got my hopes up."

"You wanted my baby?" he asked, feeling something begin to stir behind his eyes.

"Yes. I wanted your baby. Our baby. And a chance—to do it differently with ours."

"Ah, *pchelka*." He buried his head in her hair and let the tears fall, tears that hadn't fallen since the death of his mother. Maryruth had cracked open his heart, filled the darkness with her light, made him whole where he'd been broken.

She held him to her, stroking him like a child, and he *knew* he could do this.

He could be a better father than the one he'd been given.

Chapter 29

"Did you and Auggie ever talk about children?" Igor asked the next morning over breakfast.

Maryruth sat in a kitchen chair, her chin resting on her propped-up leg. In one hand was a cup of decaf coffee, the other a pencil which was poised over her sketchpad. She didn't stop her doodle when she answered.

"Yes. A few times. It came back to the same thing every time: he was a painter, first and always. He didn't have much interest in fatherhood. And I didn't think motherhood would happen for me. Five percent is almost zero, ya know?"

"And look what happened to us," he said, sipping on his own coffee.

She shrugged and smiled a small smile. "Meant to be, I guess."

"Meant to be," he repeated.

A few minutes of silence passed, the only sounds in the room were Maryruth's scribbles on paper. "You're brooding."

"No, I'm not."

"What are you thinking?"

He sighed. "Did you use—were you *with* Auggie."

She glanced up and raised an eyebrow.

"Like you're with me?" he tried to clarify.

"You mean did we use protection?" she asked bluntly.

"Yes. I guess that's what I'm asking."

"Why does it matter? Aside from health, why does it matter?"

"Guess I wanted to feel like I was different."

She rolled her eyes. "Men."

"What? What about *men*?"

She lifted her chin. "You all have this need to be where no man has ever been before. Who cares if I've slept with twenty men or two?" she snapped. "Are you really this provincial?"

He smiled slowly. "You've only been with two men?"

She glared at him. "You're missing the point."

"Am I? Why only two, Maryruth? If you believe what you say about promiscuity, why weren't you more promiscuous?"

"Because I didn't have a chance. I wasn't ready in high school, so I waited. Then I moved to the city, met Auggie. We were together for six years. And now there's you."

"And now there's me," he repeated, a smile still on his face.

She rolled her eyes, anger diffusing.

"Guess we're done fighting, *da*?"

"For now." She shrugged. "When are we telling people?"

"Not for a while yet." Their baby was a beautiful, happy surprise—for them. But it was also a complication in the world they lived in.

"Good." She looked relieved. "I want to wait. Until I'm farther along. Just in case."

He didn't offer false reassurances. Instead, he got up from the table and swept her into his arms. "Whatever happens, it happens to the both of us."

She relaxed in his embrace and leaned her head against his chest. He wanted to curl around her, protect her from the harsh truths of life, but Maryruth was strong. At eighteen, she'd left the only home she'd ever known and moved from a small town to New York. She'd done it alone, without the support of her family, and she'd made her way in the harsh, brutal city. No wonder she was so self-assured and didn't take anyone's judgments to heart.

"Plans for today?" she asked, pulling back and retaking her seat.

"Meeting with Sasha," he said. Others, too. Including Vlad and Ori. They had to move fast, and they couldn't wait much longer. "I might be out. Late."

"Late," she repeated with a slow nod. "All right."

"You just accept that from me?" he asked in amazement.

"Yes." She crossed her arms over her chest. "You have things you have to take care of. If I said to you I was going to be home late, what would you think?"

"Different. I have my family business and you have your…"

She sighed. "Yeah, fine." She pinned him with a stare. "Just family business, right? No monkey business? With some other beautiful woman?"

His laugh came from deep within the cavern of his belly. "No monkey business, I promise." Igor shoved his hands in his suit pockets and looked at her. "Tonight. When I come home to you, I might be—"

"Like the night in The Arena?"

He nodded.

"Okay."

"Okay?" he asked in hesitation.

"Okay," she repeated. "Just one thing. You come home in one piece. I don't care about anything else."

"You really mean that, don't you?"

"Wouldn't say it if I didn't mean it."

"Say something else you mean," he commanded.

"I love you."

"I know that. Say something else."

She rolled her eyes. "What else? You tell me."

"Tell me you don't have regrets."

"Back to this again?"

"Never left it."

She looped her arms around his neck and pressed her body close to his. "I have no regrets. Not now. Not ever." She kissed him, hard and fast. "Now leave."

"Don't want to," he admitted.

Maryruth smiled and gently released him. "The sooner you leave, the sooner you can come home."

"This feels like home to you?" He looked around. Sometimes, it still felt sterile. It belonged to him, but he wanted their home to belong to both of them.

"It does."

"Promise?"

She laughed and pushed against his chest. "Will you get out of here?"

He shook his head, moved back in for one quick kiss, and then went to plan the destruction of others.

Chapter 30

He came home to her feral, smelling of sweat and blood.
She didn't ask questions, nor did she ask him to bathe.
He needed her.
She took him to bed, calmed him, eased his suffering.
He felt dirty and clean when he came inside her.
She moaned her rapture.
Anguish and torment faded as the sun rose.
They slept.

Chapter 31

"Someone took out the Bosnians," Olaf said that Sunday over lunch.

"Oh?" Igor replied with nonchalance. He slathered a piece of bread with butter and took a bite. He wanted this lunch concluded quickly. The less time spent with his father, the better. He had more important things to worry about. Like finding a house outside the city.

"Chechens, too." Olaf's tone was pointed.

Igor finally looked at his father. "What are you saying?"

"I'm not saying anything." Olaf reached for his coffee. "Unless there's anything you wish to tell me."

"No. Nothing to tell."

"The Poles are worried. They think someone is moving through the Eastern European families. They think they're next."

"What do you think? Are you worried for us?"

"No. Not at this stage. Prime time to take over the other territories."

"Agreed. I'll make that happen."

"Excellent. We have a sit down with Aleksy Kowal at

the end of next week. I want to assure him that should there be any sort of trouble, we will aid them."

Igor nodded. It never hurt to have to more allies.

"Friday morning," Olaf went on.

"Friday isn't good," Igor said before he could think to stop himself.

"Why not?" Olaf demanded.

"Ah, Maryruth and I have a meeting with a realtor," he lied quickly.

"Reschedule. This is more important," Olaf snapped.

"You're right. I'll reschedule."

"No doubt she can't wait to spend your money."

Igor blinked. "Not all women want men for their money."

He snorted.

Igor didn't remind Olaf that it had been Igor's mother who'd had come into the marriage with money. Olaf had had nothing. Nothing except a vision and a thirst for power.

"Are we done here?" Igor asked.

"Always so impatient." Olaf smirked. "I suppose if I had your wife to go home to, I'd feel the same way."

It took all of Igor's resources not to punch Olaf in his sneering face. Instead, he got up and walked out of the restaurant. Igor had to remind himself that in a few weeks' time, he'd never have to look at his father's face again.

A cloud passed overhead, drenching him in shadow. He shivered. What was in store for him if he went through with this? It had to be done; he believed that. He wanted his father dead. For good, for bad, for personal reasons, for business reasons, Olaf needed to die.

But Igor realized he could not take the coward's way out. He would be the one to look into Olaf's face and pull the trigger. He would be law and executioner. When Igor led, he would never ask a soldier to do something he wouldn't do himself. It would start with his father's death.

When Igor got home, his mood had gone from sour to black. The apartment was empty. He pulled out his phone to call Maryruth.

"Come up to the roof," she said when she answered the call. Not bothering to listen to his reply, she hung up.

The sight that greeted him had his jaw dropping in disbelief. The roof was an array of colorful blooms, mostly roses. Maryruth was on her hands and knees, a large straw hat shielding her face.

"*Pchelka*," he murmured.

Looking over her shoulder, she smiled. She stood, wiping her dirty hands on her overalls. "Surprise."

"Surprise, indeed. When did you—how did you—in four days?"

She laughed. "You have your work, I have mine."

He looked around. She'd transformed the entire mass of concrete into a sanctuary.

"Come here," she said, holding out her dirt-smudged hand. He clasped it immediately. She led him through the garden, naming different types of flowers he'd never remember. He didn't look at the blooms—instead he focused on her. Her voice was filled with animation and excitement, her free hand gesturing wildly.

A pair of wicker chairs and a small glass table rested among the flowers. On the table were two glasses and a pitcher of yellow liquid. "Lemonade," she explained. "Just like Grandma Maryruth used to make. Sit. I'll pour you a glass."

He sank down onto a blue cushion and clutched the cup she handed him. He took a sip and then shook his head. It was the perfect blend of tart and sweet.

"How do you do it?" he asked.

"Do what?" she asked, running a hand underneath the brim of her hat.

"Turn my day from shit to magic."

She smiled. "Drink your lemonade." She got up and went to a purple bloom. Crouching down, she leaned over to inhale its fragrance. Her eyes closed.

If he'd had a camera, he would've snapped a thousand pictures of that moment.

Her eyes opened and she glanced at him. "What do you think of Olga?"

"For?"

"The baby."

His breath hitched.

"I know—it's getting ahead of things. There's still so much time for it to—but I was thinking, if we named her, then maybe the universe would be kind."

Igor didn't say anything for a long moment; he couldn't speak past the lump of emotion in his throat. "Olga."

Her blue eyes were bright with unshed tears. "For your mother."

"How do you know it's a girl?"

"I don't," she admitted. "But one can hope, right?"

He laughed. "And if it's a boy? Have you thought of a name?"

"Pyotr."

For his great-great grandfather, the original owner of the viola.

He set down the glass of lemonade and got up from his seat. Crouching down next to her, he removed her hat so he could touch her cheeks, feel the sun on her skin. "You would do that? For me?"

Her hand covered his. "It's no burden, Igor. It's an honor. Let's honor them."

Bowing his head, he pressed his forehead to her shoulder. He wanted to honor her, and everything she stood for.

They stayed on the roof and watched the sun set, their clasped hands resting on her flat belly, the bloom of tomorrow a whispered promise.

Chapter 32

"I can't make it to the doctor's appointment on Friday," Igor said, later that night when they were in bed together.

"Why?"

"Business meeting. Can't get out of it."

"We'll reschedule," she said.

"All right." He sighed. "I'm sorry."

"Me too. But, you have to do what you have to do, right?"

He'd give anything in the world to be able to share his burdensome thoughts with his wife, but he wouldn't bring her down too. She didn't need to worry about anything except carrying Olga to term. They'd be afraid in the coming months. Igor wouldn't breathe easily until they held a healthy baby in their arms. And then he'd worry for an entirely new set of reasons: parenthood.

"Play us something," she said.

"Hmm?" he asked in distraction.

"Play us something. Me and the baby."

"Does the baby even have ears yet?" Igor asked with a smile.

"Who cares? You're fidgeting. Play us something beautiful."

He climbed out of bed and went to retrieve his viola from the closet. He brought it back into the bedroom, unsnapped the case, and drew out the instrument. Placing it against his shoulder, he tuned the strings and then began to play. The song was a joyful one, and no one was more surprised than Igor. At the end, Maryruth clapped and demanded another. Igor played for an hour straight and when he was finished, he got back into bed, exhausted.

"That was your plan all along," he said, eyes closing.

She pressed her front to his back and spooned him. "Maybe."

"You know me, don't you?"

"Perhaps." Her lips brushed across his neck. "Go to sleep, Igor."

He fell into a deep sleep and woke up to Maryruth on top of him, kissing him awake. She was painted gold in the early morning light, her hair bright and shimmering.

Igor caressed her curves, lingering on the parts of her body that would one day soon show the life growing inside her. But she was still lean and slim, full of supple grace.

"I love you," she whispered, leaning over him.

His lips captured a nipple, and he sucked it into his mouth. Her moans of pleasure intensified his, and soon they were slick with sweat—wet heat, caught up in each other and the moment.

Maryruth collapsed on top of him. They both were breathing hard, and he heard her chuckle in his ear.

"What?" he asked, pleased at her amusement.

"I don't know. I just had this thought about one day giving Olga the birds and the bees talk and then I thought about what it's called in Russian."

It was his turn to chuckle. His hand stroked up and down her back.

"What is it called in Russian?" she wondered aloud.

"The birds and the bees. With a thicker accent."

She pinched his side. "So insolent."

"You find me charming. Admit it."

Maryruth sat up but didn't climb off him. "I do. I did. I hated you for it—when we first met."

"Things change, yes?"

She traced his bottom lip with her finger. "Yes. Yes, they do."

∽

The first time Maryruth had morning sickness, he had to leave and go to a meeting with his bastard of a father.

Igor felt like an ass.

She clutched the can of Ginger Ale as she watched him from the confines of the bed. "Not that one," she said as he picked up a three-piece gray suit. "Wear black."

"Why? I never wear my black suit."

"Black is a power color. I feel like you need to have that on your side today."

"You don't even know what the meeting is about," he pointed out.

"Black suit. White shirt. Black tie. Trust me."

He took her word for it. Fifteen minutes later, he presented himself to her. She nodded her approval.

"Hot," she claimed. "Ridiculously hot."

He laughed and then leaned over to kiss her. "Dinner tonight. Just you and me."

"And then the doctor tomorrow morning," she reminded him.

"Right." The doctor's office wasn't normally open on a Saturday, but Igor had made a call and that had been that. "Can't wait."

He kissed her again. "Take it easy today, yes?"

She nodded. "As soon as I stop throwing up, I'm going up to the roof."

"To garden?"

"No. Sketch, I think."

"Love you," he said, heading out of the bedroom.

"Love you!" she called back.

He headed out onto the Manhattan streets, focusing his mind on the coming meeting. He had to sit next to Olaf and pretend they were a united front. He climbed into his car and told his driver the address of the meeting.

Thirty minutes later, Igor was in Greenpoint and pulling up outside the travel agency. He got out of the car and looked around for Olaf's driver, but didn't see the car or the burly man who accompanied his father everywhere.

His phone chimed. Thinking it was Maryruth, he pulled it out with a smile. He frowned when he saw that it was from Olaf.

Meeting's been canceled.

With a sigh of frustration, Igor put his phone back in his pocket.

His phone chimed again.

This time it was Maryruth. It was a selfie of her up on the roof, big black sunglasses shading her eyes, a can of Ginger Ale in one hand. Just as he was about to tell his driver to turn around and take him back to the city, there was a light tap on his window. He rolled it down.

Aleksy Kowal's face filled the open window. He smiled. "Right on time."

Igor frowned. "Olaf told me the meeting was canceled."

"Yes. I know."
"What's going on?"
"Come inside the travel agency and I'll tell you."

Chapter 33

Igor settled into his seat, wondering if he'd been stupid enough to walk into a trap. Watching Aleksy's body language, Igor didn't calculate a threat. For the moment, he didn't feel the need to reach for his weapon underneath his jacket—or the one strapped to his leg.

"I don't want to do business with Olaf," Aleksy said, taking a seat on a comfortable chair across from Igor. A plate of baked goods rested on the coffee table in between them, and though they looked delicious, Igor wasn't hungry.

"You don't want to do business with Olaf," Igor repeated.

"I want to do business with *you*," Aleksy stressed. "You're innovative. I like that. I also like that you are willing to speak with me when Olaf gives me no respect. I only do business with men I respect."

Igor inclined his head in humility at the man's words. "We have a slight problem—Olaf is the head of the Russian mob. I'm just his successor."

"Yes." He paused. "Is there no way to change that?"

Igor said nothing. He didn't speak of these things with men who were not in his trusted circle. Vlad had proven himself. Sasha had been his friend since they were children.

"Would you be willing to help?" Igor asked instead.

"What do you need?"

"Nothing. At the moment."

Aleksy's eyes held Igor's. "But we have a deal, yes? From here on out, you and I conduct our business without Olaf present."

"Agreed."

The two men rose and shook hands. Just as Igor was about to leave the travel agency, Aleksy's question stopped him. "It was you, wasn't it? Behind the Bosnians and Chechens?"

Igor's mouth twisted into a rueful smile. "If it was, do you honestly believe I would take credit for that?"

Aleksy shrugged. "Some men are braggarts. Your father for instance. He's the one claiming he orchestrated it."

Igor had a lot of pride—but only about certain things. He didn't care that Olaf wanted the spotlight. Let him. Men in the spotlight were targets.

"I have no idea if Olaf was behind it," Igor lied.

"The Russians moved into their territories—fast. Something was in place. I find it hard to believe it was your father who had the foresight."

"Believe what you will, Aleksy."

With a final wave, he left the agency. His car was waiting for him and after Igor got in, he asked his driver to go for a walk. Igor wanted complete privacy to make his calls.

His first was to Sasha.

The second was to Vlad.

He told both men about the meeting that had just taken place—without Olaf. Something about it had felt off to him. Igor needed eyes on Aleksy, and he trusted Vlad to do it.

On his way home, he stopped at a flower shop and bought Maryruth a bouquet of pink roses. Though she'd been completely understanding about the change in their schedule, he hated to disappoint her.

Entering his building, he gave the doorman a wave and then headed up to the roof, not bothering to stop at the penthouse. He had a feeling she was still out in the sunshine, lingering in the warmth, daydreaming and sketching.

"Maryruth?" he called as he stepped foot onto the roof. "Maryruth, I'm back."

No reply. Was she listening to music, earbuds stuck deep in her ears so she couldn't hear anything?

He moved across the garden and turned the bend, thinking she might be sitting in one of the wicker chairs. But she wasn't there. Igor frowned. Maybe she was in the apartment taking a nap.

Just when he thought of turning back and heading inside, he saw it: an outstretched hand nestled in a cluster of tender, purple blooms.

The pink roses in his hand dropped to the ground. He ran.

Her dusky pink sundress was stained with dirt. Her wavy mass of blond hair shielded her face.

Everything around him ceased to exist.

He crouched down next to her and gently rolled her onto her back. Igor brushed the hair away from her terrified sightless eyes, her mouth open as if to call out.

But there hadn't been a chance.

The bullet to her forehead had made sure of that.

Chapter 34

Six hours later, Igor was nursing a bottle of vodka, Vlad and Sasha with him. Igor hadn't said a word, not since they'd arrived and taken in the scene. Igor hadn't yet begun to feel. To feel would annihilate him.

Maryruth had been assassinated. It was clear to all of them. Her wedding ring hadn't been removed from her finger, the delicate gold chain she wore around her neck was still there.

"Olaf," Sasha stated. "It had to have been Olaf."

"Doubt he was acting alone," Vlad added.

Igor drank more vodka.

His wife's body rested in their bed. He wasn't ready to make arrangements. Did he want a funeral? A service? He was leaning towards cremation. Her ashes could live on the mantle, and one day, when he had a rose garden on a piece of property outside the city, he'd scatter her to rest.

Morbid? Yes. He was Russian, after all.

"What should we do?" Sasha asked Igor, looking for direction.

Igor had no direction to give. He spoke through his daze. "Not sure."

"How did someone get inside?" Sasha asked. "Charlie announces visitors. There's security in place."

Igor shook his head. "Not now. I don't want to talk about this now." Leaning his head back against the couch, he closed his eyes. "Vlad, will you give me a moment with Sasha?"

Vlad slipped silently out of the apartment.

"I killed her," Igor admitted when they were alone, finally opening his eyes to look at his oldest friend.

"No," Sasha said. "You didn't."

"My life. My enemies. Couldn't protect her. Promised her I could. Promised I could protect them both." His mouth twisted in a gruesome cry of anguish.

"Both?"

"She was pregnant."

Sasha cursed in Russian. "We'll make him pay, Igor. I swear we'll make Olaf pay."

Igor shook off his frozen pain, rage blooming inside him. He took it, molded it into something hard and deadly. "I want the names of everyone who helped him. All of them. I won't stop until they're all dead."

"We'll find them," Sasha vowed. "You're not in this alone."

Igor didn't reply. Alone was the only way to live. Alone, no one could hurt him. Alone, there were no crippling losses he'd have to mourn.

He picked up Maryruth's cell phone.

"He wanted me to find her," Igor said. "I'll bet a million dollars, Aleksy Kowal is in league with Olaf. I was meant to be at the meeting alone because then she'd be unprotected."

The passcode on her phone was 1111. He had teased

her about it, saying she needed a stronger password. She laughed and said there was nothing to hide.

He looked through her emails and texts, but there was nothing there.

A vision of the bullet to her head flashed in his mind. He needed to look at a photo; he needed to see her as the vibrant, amazing woman who had changed him for the better. He had to remember her that way.

His jaw gaped when he saw all the photos she'd taken of him when he wasn't looking. Some were even of him sleeping. She'd caught him unaware, open.

Igor scrolled through the pictures from just that morning. There were views from the roof, photos of the garden, and then the selfies started. He couldn't hold in a laugh when he saw some of her more ridiculous poses.

He flipped the screen to show Sasha, who gave him a pained smile. Igor was about to turn the phone off when Sasha stopped him.

"Wait. Can I see that?"

Igor handed him the phone.

Sasha swiped through the photos, a frown marring his face. He tapped the screen, zoomed in, adjusted the brightness. He looked up at Igor. "I think I found something."

~

Igor waited at the warehouse by the docks. His impatience was getting the best of him. He'd wanted to go with Sasha and Vlad, but they'd both convinced him he wasn't in the right frame of mind for stealth. So he waited for them to bring him his prey.

He heard the low rumble of a car approaching, and knew he wouldn't be waiting much longer. Five minutes later, Vlad and Sasha tossed the bound and gagged mouth of the Polish mafia at his feet.

Aleksy Kowal's eyes were wide, afraid. He babbled incoherently behind his gag, no doubt attempting to apologize, to beg for his life.

Igor said nothing. He pulled out his weapon, screwed on a silencer, and then pressed it to the man's forehead.

"You betrayed the wrong man," he purred.

He pulled the trigger.

"Make sure he's never found," Igor said to Vlad, handing him his weapon.

The assassin nodded.

Igor looked at Sasha. "One more stop tonight."

Igor flipped on the bedroom light.

The woman bolted up and attempted to scramble from the bed. Sasha stopped her.

She was dangerous—raven hair, a mouth created for sin, a body made for a man's destruction. She knew it. And even when she found two armed men in her bedroom, she was able to fulfill the role of siren.

Igor was immune.

"What are you doing here?" she asked with a sleepy smile. "Here for a nightcap? Something more perhaps?" She looked up at Sasha. "And you brought a friend. How nice."

Sasha squeezed the back of her neck, demanding silence.

"My wife is dead," Igor said, looming over the bed.

Her face was a picture of sadness. "I'm sorry. What happened?"

"A calculating bitch managed to get past my doorman. What I want to know is how."

She looked at him in confusion. "I'm sure I have no idea."

So she wanted to play it that way, did she?

Igor pulled out Maryruth's phone and showed Katarina the photo. "Bottom right. A bright spot in the photo."

She pretended to study it. "What am I looking at?"

Igor scrolled to the next photo. "Same spot. Only this time, the sunlight didn't catch the metal of your ring."

"Why would you think it's a ring?"

"Sasha noticed the brightness in one of the photos. I wasn't sure it was anything. And then I remembered that I'd had a hidden camera installed on the roof. And I told no one—not even my best friend. The footage condemns you."

Panic flashed in her green eyes.

"So," Igor purred, loving the terror he instilled. "I'm going to ask again. How did you get past my doorman?"

She paused before answering. "I'd met him before, when you and I were… I told him I was a friend of your wife's."

"So if anyone asked if he'd seen anything unusual, he would've said no," Sasha voiced.

"Here's what I don't understand," Igor said, pretending to sound conversational. "What did you stand to gain? What did Olaf promise you?"

She blinked emerald eyes at him. "You."

"Me?"

"Marriage."

"Your father forgave me for breaking our fake engagement."

"*Da*, but there were things he wouldn't give to Olaf—not unless they were bound by marriage."

"What things?" Igor demanded.

Kat closed her mouth and looked away.

"Answer me."

"Slave trade," she whispered. "My father's in the slave trade business. Olaf wanted in."

"What was Aleksy Kowal's stake in all of this?"

"He had the space—the real estate. He'd keep the girls and—"

"Enough," Igor spat. "I've heard enough."

"You killed him?" she whispered.

"*Da*. I killed him. I kill all those who betray me." Igor paused, letting his words sink in. "She was pregnant."

Kat blanched. "I—"

Reaching out, Igor clasped Kat's slender throat in his gloved hand and began to squeeze. "She was pregnant and you murdered her."

As Kat lost the ability to breathe, her fair skin turned a blotchy red, her eyes widening in fear. At the last moment, Igor released her.

She coughed, dragging air into her lungs.

"You're going to kill me, too," she stated flatly.

"You don't deserve death," Igor stated, finally letting his wrath out of the ice cage he'd stuck it in.

He took a step closer.

"I have something worse planned for you."

She shrank back in terror.

"There are so many men who'd love to break you." He looked at Sasha. "Let's find a bidder, shall we?"

Chapter 35

The church was empty. Even men of the cloth could be bought.

Igor ducked into the confessional and waited. He didn't have to wait long. His father was punctual. As always.

Father and son, sociopath and sinner, separated by a plank of wood.

His skin prickled with rage. There was so much anger inside of him, it threatened to consume him.

Patience.

Revenge, retribution, blood. It was all his.

Olaf coughed. "Forgive me, Father, for I have sinned. It's been three days since my last confession."

Two days since Igor had found Maryruth dead. Two days since he'd murdered the head of the Polish Mafia. Two days since he'd sold Katarina Drugov to a Mexican drug lord.

"I had my son's wife murdered."

"Why?" Igor asked, pitching his tone low to sound more like Father Michael's smoker's voice.

"The woman he married was changing him. I grew

jealous and afraid that my legacy would all be undone because of a woman."

"So you believed you were acting for the greater good."

Olaf latched onto his words like a lifeline. "Yes. Yes, absolutely. All for Igor. All for the greater good."

"Recite the Act of Contrition," he commanded.

Olaf spoke the words and then ended with, "God, I have mercy."

Igor delivered the Prayer of Absolution.

At the end, Olaf said, "Amen."

"God has forgiven your sins," Igor said, rising. Before Olaf had a chance to leave, Igor kicked through the confessional partition, grabbed his father by his suit lapels, and hauled him close so they were nose to nose.

"God has forgiven your sins," Igor spat into Olaf's terrified face, "but I haven't."

"Igor," Olaf begged.

Igor dragged the blade slowly across his father's throat.

"Son—"

The word ended on a gurgle.

Igor cast Olaf's body aside and spat on his form.

He stepped out of the confessional, covered in his father's blood, and sheathed the blade to his ankle. When he came to the front doors of the church, he kicked them open, all respect, all honor, gone.

There was no one left to honor anyway.

Sasha and Vlad stood on the stone steps and moved to flank him.

Igor Dolinsky looked down on the streets of Manhattan.

He clenched his fists. "Let's take this fucking city."

Epilogue
SIX YEARS LATER

Gripping his glass of vodka, Igor swore he heard his dead wife's laugh.

His head whipped around to stare at the woman on stage.

The auburn-haired siren captured every man's attention as she performed her burlesque number.

Throwing her head back, she laughed again as her hands glided down the length of her body.

Not his wife.
Another.
Different.
Igor wanted her.
She was his.
Only she didn't know it yet.

Additional Works

The Tarnished Angels Motorcycle Club Series:

Wreck & Ruin (Tarnished Angels Book 1)
Crash & Carnage (Tarnished Angels Book 2)
Madness & Mayhem (Tarnished Angels Book 3)
Thrust & Throttle (Tarnished Angels Book 4)
Venom & Vengeance (Tarnished Angels Book 5)
Fire & Frenzy (Tarnished Angels Book 6 - Pre-Order)

SINS Series:

Sins of a King (Book 1)
Birth of a Queen (Book 2)
Rise of a Dynasty (Book 3)
Dawn of an Empire (Book 4)
Ember (Book 5)
Burn (Book 6)
Ashes (Book 7)
Fall of a Kingdom (Book 8)

Additional Works

Others:

Peasants and Kings

About the Author

Wall Street Journal & USA Today bestselling author Emma Slate writes romance with heart and heat.

Called "the dialogue queen" by her college playwriting professor, Emma writes love stories that range from romance-for-your-pants to action-flicks-for-chicks.

When she isn't writing, she's usually curled up under a heating blanket with a steamy romance novel and her two beagles—unless her outdoorsy husband can convince her to go on a hike.

Made in United States
Troutdale, OR
08/04/2023

11740203R00116